PENGUIN BOOKS

NISANIT

Fadia Faqir was born in Amman in 1956. She gained her
BA in English Literature and MA in Creative Writing at,
respectively, Jordan University and Lancaster University.
Fadia Faqir is at present working on her second novel while
pursuing a doctorate in Creative Writing at the University of
East Anglia.

This novel is dedicated to:

My parents:
Ahmad Al-Faqir and
Samiha Bayyouka

My teacher:
Anthony Crocker

My friends:
Sana Aloul and
Amal Ghandour

Acknowledgements

I am deeply indebted to Prof. David Craig of Lancaster University for his great contribution to this novel. I also appreciate the sincere critiques of my class mates especially Ailsa Cox, Adrienne Brady and John Miller. Many thanks to Sue Blackwell who showed immense patience while typing the manuscript. I am also indebted to Lancaster University Library staff who facilitated my research with their efficiency and understanding. Finally, I would like to express my gratitude to the British Council for financing the M.A. course.

FADIA FAQIR
Nisanit

PENGUIN BOOKS

PENGUIN BOOKS

Published by the Penguin Group
27 Wrights Lane, London W8 5TZ, England
Viking Penguin Inc., 40 West 23rd Street, New York, New York 10010, USA
Penguin Books Australia Ltd, Ringwood, Victoria, Australia
Penguin Books Canada Ltd, 2801 John Street, Markham, Ontario, Canada L3R 1B4
Penguin Books (NZ) Ltd, 182–190 Wairau Road, Auckland 10, New Zealand

Penguin Books Ltd, Registered Offices: Harmondsworth, Middlesex, England

First published by Aidan Ellis Publishing Ltd 1987
Published in Penguin Books 1988

Printed and bound in Great Britain by
Cox & Wyman Ltd, Reading

Nisanit

Occupied Palestine/the Democratic State of Israel

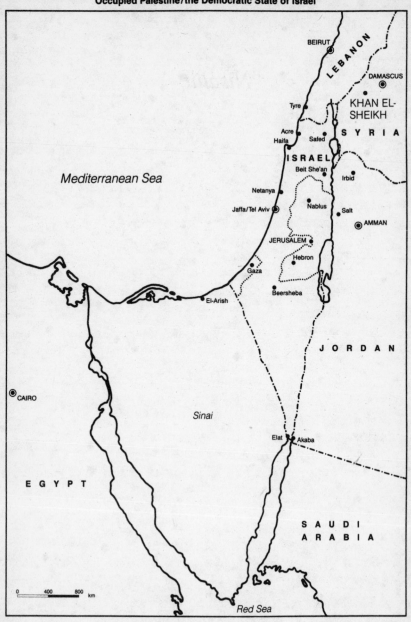

PART ONE

The Democratic State of Ishmael – Rahmah – 1969

Bang. Bang. The soldier forced the door open and entered our home. He was followed by other soldiers wearing their brownish-green uniforms and carrying rifles in their hands. At the end of each barrel a shining piece of metal was fixed. It was like the kitchen knife Mummy used to cut cake with. Mummy's smiling face turned blue. She snatched my hand and said, 'Eman, come here. Take these leaflets quickly to Um-Musaad's house.' They were packed in a bale. I took it and ran as quickly as I could down the stairs. Thinking a little about the whole thing, I realized that I would have to take a short cut and climb the Farahs' wall. My heart was beating like the cloth-shredding machine which used to come to our neighbourhood. I almost dropped the bale, but I felt vaguely that that would be awful. Grasping the leaflets firmly with my fingers I reached our neighbour's door. Um-Musaad knew what was going on, so she pulled me inside. I was gasping when she snatched the bale out of my hands and cut the rope. She started unpicking pillow cases and hiding the papers in them and stitching them up again. She raised the head of her old ill father-in-law with her hands and replaced his pillows with the stuffed ones. 'When you go out, don't answer any questions! Do you hear?' she said. I would talk to no one. I had lost my tongue.

When I went back home, my usually calm Mummy was howling and Daddy was putting on his festival suit. It was dark blue. Daddy was a very elegant man. He never left the house with a hair out of place or without a tie. This time his shirt was unbuttoned.

The soldiers were turning the house upside down: opening drawers, tearing pillows and mattresses . . . My cloth doll was lying on the floor. Mummy had made it for me out of the pieces she could spare from her few dresses. I was looking at Lulu, the first and last doll I ever had, and praying that they wouldn't see it. One officer caught my eyes and very slowly inserted the point edge of his rifle-blade inside its belly. Struck with pain, I started weeping silently. I went to our bedroom and sat in the corner. A soldier entered the room and stepped with his black boots on our mattresses and sheets. He began turning them upside-down and then tearing them.

I heard the noise coming from outside so I went out to join the family. All our neighbours were standing by their windows watching Daddy, handcuf-fed, being dragged to the army vehicle. Daddy's face was white, his lips were blue, but his features were swathed in serenity. He looked at us for the last time and disappeared inside the huge vehicle. A soldier was carrying a transistor with an antenna. He talked to it saying, 'From 235 to 03. Answer.'

'03, yes,' the transistor answered.

'Rahmah. The Democratic State of Ishmael. 22nd November 1969. Sir, at 5.25 we arrested the conspirator Mohammed Saqi, second man of the National Freedom Party.'

'235, well done.'

'Sir, Operation 4, done.'

The air smelled of sweat, tears and blood. It was not a nightmare because the fingertips of the soldiers could be seen all over our cosy house. They killed Lulu. Didn't they? Shocked and frightened, I sat in the corner of our bedroom crying all night long.

*

'Official announcement number three: This is Radio Ishmael broadcasting from Rahmah. Dear listeners everywhere, the courageous armed forces have aborted an attempt to overthrow our loyal Government. Seventeen members of the destructive National Freedom Party were arrested in a comb-and-sweep operation of the public areas of the capital. The loudspeaker of the armed forces headquarters has made known the names of all the members of the Party. If you are familiar with any of them, please notify the nearest Police Station. Serve your God. Serve your country. Serve your ruler.'

Occupied Palestine – Nablus – 1984

Darkness, the natural ally of the guerilla fighter, surrounded Shadeed, enveloped him, protected him like a loving mother. Four more hours of marching and that night's training would be over. He raised his legs high, then placed them carefully on the ground, as if pedalling to avoid tumbling over a rock or a tree trunk. Al-Nar mountain stood erect against the blackish sky and appeared to him high, higher than usual. The sweat trickling down his chest and back cooled his hot body. Sticky cold. He was afraid that HQ had changed their minds and no longer intended to send him on a mission. No orders, although it was the beginning of June. He was fed up with looking down the length of his machine-gun. They fooled the Zionists, confused them. Intelligence would trace the Fedayeen who did that soon. Bloody efficient. Men and faith win wars, not machinery. He lay down on the ground and pressed his belly to the soil which he loved. The Zionists had stolen it. His knapsack was heavy and the stones inside pierced his skin. He crawled along the mountainside making sure that his limbs were bent like a frog. When he reached the bottom, the skin covering his elbows and knees blazed with pain. He sat down on a rock, took his blouse off and wiped his forehead. Stirred by the faint light that brightened the sky of Nablus, the sparrows and pigeons started cooing and twittering. He emptied the sack and jogged back home.

He had improved since he began his training last January, when the HQ told him that they wanted him to be a combatant Fedayee. The letter they sent him was brief and to the point. 'You are welcome to join the Revolution army as a combatant Fedayee. Start day and night marches. Read the books that will be soon given to you by one of your brothers. Arrangements for smuggling arms have been made. Long live a free Palestine. Revolution until victory.' As long as he could remember he had been a non-combatant Fedayee, recruiting, delivering messages, arranging contacts. The thought of fighting filled his heart with pride. He would restore their dignity, not just by carrying out secure auxilliary missions, but by walking under the fire. He would stand on the verge of the bubbling volcano and share with his brothers the honour of fighting for Palestine.

His mother would be sleeping under his father's picture, her favourite spot. He pushed the door gently.

'Shadeed?' she asked.

'Hajjeh Amina, my mother, you still can't sleep properly?'

'No, my son. Samir came and gave me this paper.'

He read the message quickly. Margerite-bride-stone. The code they invented last summer. Zero-start-six. The order he had been waiting for. He sighed and burnt the paper. Tomorrow morning they would launch the planned attack.

'What does he want?'

'Nothing. Try to go to sleep.'

He looked at the empty Cola bottles lined up in the closet and took out two. The campaign to clean the market place organized by the Tel-Al-Asaker Refugee Camp Youth was designed mainly for this reason.

Empty cans and bottles. The sun would rise soon. He'd better hurry. Kerosene three parts and motor oil one. The heavy liquid gurgled down the bottles. Three Molotovs were ready. He checked the time. 0430. He removed some pots and pans, slid back a wooden board, then dug out some soil until he touched the cloth covering the machine-gun. Drenched in oil, the cloth gleamed in the twilight. When he touched the cold metal, a strange tremor ran through his body. He would use it for the first time that morning. He looked down the length of the barrel at an imaginary target. How many times had he done that? He wanted to ease the safety catch off and press the trigger. He felt like a football player kept behind the line for too long. Other players messed up clean passes that he would definitely have put straight into the goal.

He opened the wooden box and pulled out his father's army uniform. Tough material. 'Made in Great Britain' was stamped into the rubber where the sole of the boot met the heel. He had probably taken them from a dead British soldier during the days of the Mandate. He kissed the boot and placed it next to the uniform on the box.

He heated some water and washed his body. While rubbing his thighs with soap, he remembered Eman. He needed her badly. If she had been there that night, he would definitely have made love to her. Sad eyes. He dried himself and put on a thick cotton jumper, the shirt and trousers of his father, thick stockings, then slipped his feet into the boots and tied the laces. He fixed the ammunition belt around his waist and tied the tail rope. How long would the operation take? Three days?

0600 –	A car would take them from the camp to Hebron. Sheikh Masaud would make sure that the driver was both deaf and mute.
0815 –	Hide in the building under construction.
0910 –	The committee would leave the building on the opposite side. Shoot armed settlers.
0920 –	Jump into the car.
1023 –	Hide in the commercial centre.
2300 –	Drive back to Nablus. Hide in the mountains and wait there for further orders.

Hiding in the commercial centre for that long was too dangerous. Surely it was not a complete plan? How many days were they supposed to spend in the mountains?

The sound of a horn woke him up. He put on his jacket, wrapped the white and black head-dress around his neck, picked up the machine-gun and the sack, kissed his mother's cheek and rushed out. Her voice followed him, 'May God be with you. Amen.'

He jumped in next to Adnan and they drove off.

'The head-dress, Shadeed. Take it off. If they see it . . .'

'Yes,' he said and pushed it into the sack, almost reluctant to hide the symbol of the P.L.O.

'If we are lucky none of the bastards will stop us,' said the driver.

Shadeed looked at him. He was neither deaf nor mute. 'If they do, you know what to do,' he said cuttingly.

The driver nodded.

Samir said, 'Deeds, deeds speak louder than words.' He was in a talkative mood. He made a gesture that meant silence, then straightened his back and looked out of the window. Talking would waste their energy. If a soldier stopped them, they must shoot. Killing soldiers at check points was not his idea of guerilla fighting. It would be less significant than killing members of the Settlers' Committee. The first would be 'an operation', while the second would be, as Che put it, a means to achieve an end. Settlements were the hottest danger. The operation might check the settlements that flooded his country and make the settlers' radical army think twice before killing innocent Arab students. He tightened the laces of his boots. His hands were shaking. Fear? Excitement?

'We're approaching Hebron. Sneak into the building. The guard is RM, don't worry.'

So the guard was a member of the resistance movement! Not bad, people of Hebron. The car stopped suddenly. They strolled into the three-storey building, their base for the next hour. It was just a skeleton, no doors, windows or finishings. They went up to the third floor. The room facing the street was full of cement sacks. Samir rushed in, but he grabbed his shoulder. 'You fool. They might see you.' They crawled along and calmly piled the sacks on top of each other to form a barricade. 'We will shoot squatting. Leave holes for eyes and barrels.'

Nine o'clock exactly: everything was ready. He took off his jacket, folded it and sat on it. He rolled up his sleeeves and watched the main gate of the building. His hands were wet.

Samir rubbed his hands and said, 'A little bit of action makes the man younger.'

'Action to achieve an end. Also, it makes the man older,' said Adnan.

Shadeed eased back the safety catch of the slick Galilee.

The Democratic State of Ishmael – Rahmah – 1969

It must have been related to the paper I read when I wanted to take my pocket money from Daddy's trousers. It was written in fading red. It said, 'The armoured division will occupy the Radio Station at zero hour. The militia will blow up the railway bridge simultaneously.' I had never told anyone about this paper because I felt that I was stepping on forbidden ground. The last ten days of Ramadan, Daddy stopped coming back home. But the first day of the feast, he showed up carrying bags of fruit and a green plastic sword for my youngest brother. Smiling, he kissed and hugged us one by one, but I felt that there was something wrong. Three days later he was taken by the soldiers. I kept crying and asking for him until Mummy hit me with what she had in her hand, a spoon. She had never done that before.

My best friend, Tal'at, stopped arguing with me and became nicer. At school all my friends stopped talking to me, so in the break I used to sit at my desk slowly chewing my sandwich. Instead of eating fruit every day and most of the time refusing Mummy's offer of an orange, we started asking for some. She used to say that our uncle was the head of the family. He was always so busy and could not buy things for us. After that I stopped being keen on any kind of food, as if, by tearing Lulu, the soldier had taken

17

part of my stomach. But my baby sister's stomach was all right. She kept crying for food and nobody took any notice of her. Even when Mummy breastfed her occasionally, she went on yelling because Mummy's breasts were thin and limp.

'They tried a coup, but failed,' I heard my aunt, Hanin, saying to Mummy one morning. I could not understand the word, but I knew that Daddy had done something really big. Our house was full of relatives who sat looking at each other's faces.

'Don't worry, things will get back to normal again,' said Tal'at. 'Let's cook petals in empty cans.' He knew that this was my favourite game.

At 0910, some members of the Settlers' Committee left the building opposite. Shadeed saw the rifles dangled carelessly across their shoulders. An attack was not expected. No informers that time. Through the opening he saw every tiny detail. The skullcapped crowd hurried to their cars, but one called them back to tell them a joke. They cracked up with laughter. Laughing at Arabs, of course. The faces of the murdered students rushed across the chatting crowd. His voice was hoarse when he gave the order, 'Ready, inflict the heaviest possible casualties – shoot!'

He pulled the cold trigger. A burst of automatic fire sprayed the pavement. They stood still for a second, then threw themselves clumsily down. He pointed and fired at one of them who tumbled like a brick. The metal bullet swung him upwards, then pushed him downwards. He had killed one of them, but he was not thrilled, happy or even excited. 'Cover me,' he said and wrapped the head-dress around his face. They fired back. He jumped on top of the sacks and lit the fuse of a Molotov, then threw it as far as possible. A huge flame burst, followed by a dull explosion. A bullet whizzed by. The fluff on his earlobes bristled up – the bastards must have seen him. He pressed his belly hard along the sacks and continued lighting the Molotovs and throwing them. Zero visibility, so he just tossed them blindly through the flames and smoke. He leaped down and gazed through the hole. Two charred corpses stirred in the black cloud. Samir finished off one and Adnan the other.

'Let's go.' He tightened the head-dress around his nose. The nauseating smell of burnt flesh and hair filled the air. A strange weakness ran through his legs. He picked up the sack with a limp hand and rushed out of the building. His brothers were right behind him. The car was waiting. They jumped in and drove off to the commercial centre. It was 1025. How many had been killed in those two extra minutes?

'Take off your head-dresses. You want to ruin my youth?' the driver said. He must have been at least forty.

They laughed nervously. He wanted to scream and jump, but courageous guerilla fighters laugh when they kill the enemy, so instead he laughed and laughed until his tears ran on his cheeks.

The driver dropped them in the middle of the busy centre. It was difficult to walk between the barrows of vegetables. Each hawker spread out his boxes and sang a phrase about the kind of vegetable he sold. What if one of these Arabs were an informer?

'Come, come, come. Look, look, look. Aubergine.'

'Tomato like jewels.'

'Babies' fingers, cucumber.

'Swims in the pool, cucumber.

'Shirm-birimboo, cucumber.'

The songs got mixed, increasing the patternlessness of the crowded place.

A peasant touched Shadeed's shoulder and whispered, 'This way.' He pushed some boxes aside and led them through a passage leading to a small shelter that might take five persons if they lay down next to each other. 'Stay here,' he said and went away.

He shivered because the hole was cold after the steaming market place. When did they manage to dig this shelter? A misted clay jar, covered with a plate with a metal cup on top, invited him to drink. He gulped down some water, then passed the cup to Adnan. He shook his head. His skin was drained of blood and looked like wax. What was wrong with him?

'Give me the cup,' asked Samir in a shaky voice.

The shelter must have been used often. The water was fresh. Some bread and tomatoes were piled on a tray near the jar. 'Would you like some?' he asked Adnan. Again he shook his head.

Outside that dark dump, the market-place bustled with activity. Especially after the operation. Helicopters, patrol cars, possibly tanks, infantry and most definitely ambulances. He wondered how many they had killed. Destroy in order to build. Samir fiddled with his Galilee, too jumpy to lie down. 'Hey, relax.'

'I can't, I pulled that trigger too many times to keep my finger off it. I want to go on shooting.'

When you started walking down that road, it was almost impossible for you to turn back. The armed settlers were not human beings. Aggressors, occupiers, colonialists, killers, but not humans. You stopped respecting the gift of life when a piece of metal could take it away.

The same peasant came back that night. Without opening his mouth he took them to the car. When they settled in their seats the driver said, 'You should have seen the chaos! The air force, infantry, police, intelligence – they all got mixed up together. One of

21

the intelligence officers told the cucumber hawker to shut up. He was damn close to your hiding place, the sweat was trickling into my eyes!'

'How many?' asked Samir.

'Hard to tell.'

When they arrived at Nablus, they marched to Al-Nar mountain, the revolutionaries' haven which rarely failed the people of Palestine. Holding each other's tails, they crawled along the mountainside. He couldn't see the tip of his nose, but he knew the way to the cave by heart. Nablus was asleep and breathing evenly. Adnan was still shaken and that worried him. 'Hurry up,' he said, sliding his thighs on the stones.

'I can't. The sack is too heavy,' whispered Adnan.

'Give it to me, kiddo,' said Samir.

'I can bloody carry my own sack,' Adnan exploded.

'Then, kiddo, stop complaining.'

Between crawling, creeping, sliding, stumbling and swearing, it took them half an hour to cover the distance to the cave. He pushed back the rock and they marched inside.

'Congratulations,' he said and loosened the straps of the knapsack.

'Don't be too jubilant. The operation hasn't finished yet.'

'The major part has. We'll stay here until things cool down, then we'll go home and live happily ever after.'

'It sounds like a winter's tale,' said Adnan.

'You know,' said Samir, who was still carrying his sack, 'last month's operation screwed up right at the end. They discovered Husam's hiding place in a few hours. Efficient, they are.'

The weakness was still in his legs. An ugly existence, when you lived with fear and saw it in the faces of people around you. There was nothing heroic about

22

them. They were three trembling men who smelled badly. He touched Adnan's shoulder and asked him, 'Are you all right, my brother?'

'Yes, Shadeed,' the dry whitish lips said.

Samir went on talking about what possessed him that moment. 'They killed four of them and dragged Husam along like a rabbit. They use methods that force the peasants to spill the beans.' The peasant they had seen that morning was almost mute. The perfect non-combatant RM.

'Nobody knows where we are.'

'Except our connection. Each has a limit . . .'

'Will you knock it off,' he said, looking at Adnan's face. He was still suffering from shock.

They lit a fire to warm the cave up, and Shadeed heated some beans. 'Are you hungry?' he asked.

'Starving,' answered Samir.

'Dip the bread in the sauce. It's delicious,' he said to Adnan.

'Cheers for Uncle Sam's beans,' said Samir and they laughed.

Samir lay down on his back and tapped his belly. 'I feel better now. I'm like a tiger, I need food all the time.'

He washed the pan with some water from his canteen and stuck it in the sack. He sat down on his blanket. Through the smoke, he looked at Adnan's blurred baby-face. He wasn't tough enough. His poorly-fitting garments made him look so skinny. The second-hand clothes of Americans shipped to Palestinian refugeees would not fit the thin. That was the difference between the haves and the have-nots. His boots, which were from UNRWA too, rested on the mud. The Galilee machine-gun was pressed between his knees. He gazed at the flames thoughtfully. Samir was his foil. His strong determined chin said everything about him. Guerilla warfare reflects, in Mao's words, 'man's admirable qualities as well as his less pleasant ones.' Samir personified man's 'less pleasant ones'. He was tall and bulky. A boxer ready to jump into the arena. He counted the bullets he had.

'Shit,' he said angrily, 'I want a Kalashnikov or even better a Katyusha.'

'You're fighting on unfavourable terrain,' said Adnan.

'And what's that supposed to mean?'

'It means that we're lucky to have these Galilees and Molotovs. You know that they were smuggled from 48 Palestine, which is a victory in itself,' he said, picking up his gun and looking out of the cave's mouth. Nothing unusual. The coos and twitters of pigeons and sparrows. How many years had passed since he had heard that sound? His unshaven chin was bristly. Eman's sad eyes slid across the whitish sky. He always went to the extreme. His love for her squeezed his heart. In love and hate. He took the dreams, beliefs, illusions of a human being in one pull of a trigger. A God of some sort but with dirty nails. His hands smelt of kerosene. Better wash them or even the most stupid dog would be able to trace him. If they found them, they must not expect any mercy. He had heard what they did to Husam. They filled his pure country with dirt. He turned his head. Nablus was lying like a babe in the valley's lap. The window shields of houses glittered in the sunrise. A palm full of diamond dust. Occasionally, the heavy silence that swathed the valley was broken by the bleating of sheep. The gentle breeze of June touched his face lightly, carrying to his nostrils the smell of thyme and citrus flowers. Painful love for his home town stirred in his chest. Those golden-green

24

meadows were his blessing and his curse. He became so impatient at times. Tolerance was a luxury he couldn't afford. Why the Palestinians? Why their land?

'Shadeed, please come here. We don't want to take any chances.'

'Yes. I'm coming,' he said emphatically.

When he saw Adnan's waxen face he asked, 'You look so sad, my brother, what's wrong?'

'I don't know. It must be this damp place,' answered Adnan.

'We'll go home tomorrow.'

'Whenever I look at the flames, I see my daughter's eyes. I haven't seen her for six months. God only knows what they did to her and her mother.'

'Don't give me this bullshit. You knew that when you joined the Movement. Didn't you?' said Samir.

'How old is she?' asked Shadeed, ignoring what Samir had said.

'This year is 1984. Isn't it? I keep forgetting that. In September, she'll be two years old.'

'You'll see her soon. I'm sure.'

'I am not sure of anything any more.'

'When you join the Revolution, you give all. It's as simple as that,' said Samir heatedly.

'Yes you have to give all, but we are flesh and blood after all. Don't blame Adnan.'

'Either you're men or pampered babies in diapers.'

Samir's words echoed in the empty cave and then the heavy silence dropped again, piercing his ears. He looked at their faces and realized that sitting in that cave was neither simple nor easy. Adnan sighed, put his head on the sack and wrapped himself in his blanket. 'I am exhausted, tired to the bones,' he said, then closed his eyes.

'I'm not tired,' said Samir, but all the same he stretched himself out on the stones.

'Who's on duty tonight?' He stopped talking and listened carefully. A loud noise broke the silence. Shattered him. It must be his imagination. It took him seconds to recognize the revolving rotor blades of a helicopter. Hovering over the mountain? He picked up his Galilee and shouted, 'My brothers, they're coming.'

'Who? Who?' screamed Adnan.

The Democratic State of Ishmael – Rahmah – 1969

On Friday, Mummy decided to take me with her to visit Daddy. She cooked his favourite meal, stuffed courgette and aubergine. We carried the pot and walked down to the bus-stop where we took a bus to the army camp. Over the noise of the engine, Mummy's voice came: 'When you see him please don't cry or look frightened. Your father has changed a lot. Your smile will put some warmth into his tired heart.' Looking at the unfamiliar scenery through the window, I knew I had to change.

A soldier standing in a wooden hut near the gate of the camp asked, 'What is that?'

'Some food for my husband,' Mummy answered.

'Go to the inspection room.'

We entered a small room. A big woman was sitting on a chair. She opened Mummy's handbag and looked into it, then passed her hands over Mummy's body. 'Come, your turn,' she said to me. She passed her bulky hands over my shivering body. I took Mummy's hand and walked behind a barbed wire fence. Our hands by our sides and the pot by Mummy's legs, we stood there waiting for Daddy.

A man wearing a wide robe came towards us. Not Daddy. But when I looked at his face, I recognized his eyes. He was so thin and pale. His hair was covered with white. What had they done to him?

'Eman, Mamma.' That was what he used to call me when we played. My heart started to move up to my neck and wanted to come out of my eyes. I stopped it then and there. The lump is still in my throat to this day.

'You're growing up quickly, my little girl,' he said. I stretched my body to look taller. 'I might not come back, so please take good care of your mother. OK?'

'Yes, Daddy,' I answered with a shaky voice.

He looked at me closely. His loving eyes ran over me slowly. I managed a smile and he smiled back. It was as good as a hug. 'Love you, princess. Take care.'

He stared at Mummy, then asked her about Amal, Omar, Malik and Bakir.

'They're all all right. What we need is having you among us.'

He started talking about money matters. Mummy was complaining about someone's behaviour. I couldn't understand clearly what they were talking about. All I knew about money matters was: my pocket money was cut down from five to two piasters.

Mummy tried to give Daddy the pot. A soldier kicked it with his boot. The tomato sauce was spilt on the ground. The stuffed courgette and aubergine were scattered here and there. Mummy's eyes were full of tears when she asked, 'Why?'

'You're not allowed to hand him anything.'

Daddy looked hurt but didn't say anything. Mummy took my hand and wiped her tears with the end of her black veil.

'It's better if you go home now,' said Daddy. Mummy nodded.

Standing behind the barbed wire, Daddy looked older and miserable. He waved to us. Two soldiers came towards him and pushed him back to the old building. Carrying the empty pot, we walked out of the camp. During the trip back home, Mummy was so quiet. 'Mummy, don't be sad. He'll come back and you'll be able to cook him as many meals as you like.' She hugged me, then kissed my forehead. I moved closer to her and put my head on her chest.

The Democratic State of Israel – Nablus – 1984

The intelligence officer's information had shown that he must turn left, then go up the hill. Last night's patrol had reported unusual activities in that part of Nablus, which was almost deserted. A rural house was the only sign of humanity that could be seen. An old woman came out and started feeding the chickens. Her embroidered black dress swept the ground, providing a constant contact with the earth. The scene of the small house, the chickens and the peasant woman in the creeping sunrise was engraved on his mind. A timeless canvas. He cleared his throat and said, 'Good morning.' Good Arabic language plus the right social behaviour were the keys to his success.

She shielded her eyes and said, 'Good morning, my son.' Assessing his shabby appearance?

'I am starving, my mother. Could you give me something to eat?'

'Sure. I'll bring you a glass of goat's milk and some bread. Sit down.'

He sat down near the door and leaned against the wall. That breed was dignified and generous, but simple-minded. She must have taken him for an Arab: maybe because he had come to this area alone? She milked a goat, staring at him, then went inside the house. He must convince her that he was an Arab. The real battle was between them and the peasants, who were clever and strong.

'Eat, my son.'

The milk was still warm. Delicious, fresh stuff. He forgot why he was there until she asked, 'You have a strange accent.'

He smiled and said, 'I'm not from this area.'

'From where?'

'Gaza.'

'I see.'

'Mother, could you give me some more?' he asked like a mischievous child.

'My eyes are for you, my son,' she said kindly, then brought him more milk, bread, and some home-made butter.

'What brought you to this area?'

'Something very important.' Down to business because she tied her white veil in a knot and stuck the hem of the long dress in her belt, uncovering bright green trousers. 'I don't know if I can trust you. Forgive me, my mother. It's rather important. The lives of young men are not a joke.' He was sure now that he saw some fear in her glassy eyes. She knew something about the terrorists.

'I have to trust you. Look, I'm a member of the Resistance Movement.'

She crossed her legs and folded her hands. 'God bless you.'

That grandmother supported the RM. He would make sure that she was invited to the station. Wasn't she a little bit old to play with young kids?

'Three of our brothers are hiding somewhere here. I have a verbal message from the HQ to say they must leave the cave immediately. The Israelis will attack them one hour from now.' Her face was expressionless when he finished talking, as if it were carved from stone. Dry skin and impenetrable eyes.

She scratched her eye-lid with her finger and said, 'I don't know what you're talking about.'

'The three will be killed.'

'Which three?'

'Mother, I beg you.'

'Do you want more food?'

'No.'

'Then, God be with you, go on your way.'

The sweat clung to the grey wisps of hair that escaped the white veil. He stood up and went down the hill. There were two alternatives: either she would believe him and then she would go to them to deliver the message, or she wouldn't believe him. If so, she would run to their hiding-place to warn them. She must be their connection. Never underestimate a peasant. He squatted behind a rock, took out his field-glasses, map and walkie-talkie, then watched the house carefully. She rushed outside, then went inside the house four times in three minutes. She rubbed her hands, fixed the veil, then went inside again. After twenty minutes of running in circles around the house, he saw her throw away whatever was in her hand, tie a bundle of sticks onto her head and go up the mountain.

He pressed the button on the walkie-talkie and said, '490 calling. 490 calling.'

'04. Yes 490.'

'I think we found our baby. Storm 53 mountain. Now. 04 NOW.'

'Roger 490.'

The Democratic State of Ishmael – Rahmah – 1969

One day Mummy woke me up very early. 'Eman you're not going to school today,' she said. She was wearing her black dress and black veil. She dragged me out of bed and dressed me quickly. My aunt came running through the kitchen door in her Turkish mulaya. She used to put on her mulaya when she didn't want to be recognized. Um-Musaad joined the group. We took a taxi to somewhere called the 'Prime Ministry.'

'I hope that all the women will be there,' said Um-Musaad, 'We need big numbers.'

The 'Prime Ministry' turned out to be a huge building surrounded by high walls. Wherever I looked, I saw soldiers carrying rifles in their hands. Two jeeps were parked in front of the main gate. When the dark guards saw us, they aimed their rifles at us. Oh, if they fired we would all be dead. My hands started shaking and I wanted to pee too.

'We want our husbands! We want our fathers! We want our brothers!' shouted the women.

My aunt stuck her hand out of the black mulaya and slapped me on my back. 'Say something. Don't just stand there.'

'I want Daddy,' I said and began crying.

'The-Prime-Minister' the women repeated together, stamping rhythmically on the tarmac.

Um-Musaad tried to break through the soldiers' line. One of them struck her with his fist. She kicked him. 'You whore,' he shouted and punched her on the jaw. She hit back. Mummy gasped and together with other women attacked the soldiers. They pushed me and I fell down, but Mummy pulled me up. Another woman fell to the ground, winded. The crowd stepped on her, shouting at the soldiers, 'Prostitutes of the government.' The fight raged on. I was trapped between people's legs. Tears and blood. Blood, legs and tears.

A respectable man came out of the building and waved his hand. The soldiers obeyed and stepped back, releasing the women. Three were lying on the tarmac, among them Um-Musaad.

'Um-Musaad,' I called. She opened her eyes, stood up and clenched her fist.

'The fucking bloody soldiers.'

'Just one woman,' the Prime Minister said.

A fat ugly woman, who claimed to be my grand-mother, took my hand. The pink scarf she was wearing hardly covered her grey hair. She dragged me up the stairs. When she got quite close to him, she began crying, 'He is my only son, my master. I trust in God and then in you. Forgive them, God will forgive you.' She sat on the floor and started swaying and howling, then she pushed me down by his feet saying, 'Look at his innocent children.'

'I'll do what I can,' he said firmly. His suit was dark blue like Daddy's.

I looked at him with tearful eyes and said in a thin voice, 'Please, Uncle –' I wanted to ask him to take me to the loo. I wanted a pee badly.

'Yes. I'll do my best,' he interrupted me.

A soldier pushed us back into the dishevelled crowd. The women wiped their tears and blood.

Mummy gave the ugly woman a five-dinar piece, then we took the bus back to our neighbourhood.

When I was in the loo, I heard Mummy saying, 'Nothing will move them. They are made of stone!'

'What next?' asked my aunt, Hanin, taking off her mulaya.

'Stuffing their bellies with rice and meat. A lot of meat. What else?' said Um-Musaad, tensing her jaw.

I went to our bedroom. Every member of the family had a big drawer to put their clothes and books in. I pulled Lulu out of mine and tried to stitch her belly, but the torn fabric was so tight that she couldn't be mended.

My baby sister, Amal, was growing thin and pale. Her navel stood out because she was so skinny. Her eyes were big and gazing. She used to smile when I fondled her navel. Gradually, she stopped accepting Mummy's breast. Mummy was so worried. She didn't know what to do. 'I know that she's very ill, but I can't take her to the doctor. I don't have enough money,' she said. She went to the bedroom, picked Amal up and tried to breast-feed her. Then she looked out of the window. Rubbing her hands, she said, 'Where's your uncle? Oh God! Where is he?' Amal's colour began to change. 'Go and ask Um-Musaad to come.' I ran to our neighbour's house. 'My sister Amal. My sister Amal,' I gasped.

Um-Musaad was shredding parsley. She jumped and said, 'What's happened? Tell me what's happened!' I couldn't tell her, I had lost my tongue.

She put on her scarf and ran with me.

'She's so dark and cold and she won't suck my nipple,' Mummy explained.

'Bend her limbs and say "In the name of God",' said Um-Musaad. 'Bring me an onion.' She squeezed it – her hand was above Amal's nose – till the juice started dripping in my sister's nose. Nothing. Um-Musaad started slapping Amal, then she opened her mouth. Amal did not cry. Again Um-Musaad bent her hands, her legs. Nothing. Mummy was struck with horror. She stared at my sister.

'God help you. She's dead.'

Amal was dead! What was that supposed to mean? It must be something dreadful, because Um-Musaad was slapping her cheeks and Mummy had fallen to the ground. I rushed out of the room, hugged Lulu and began weeping silently.

After Amal's death, Mummy stopped eating. She used to sit for hours looking out of the window at the high brown mountains. I wanted my old Mummy back, so one day I said to her, 'Mummy, I love you and I want to see your smile.' She hugged me and started sobbing. I kissed her hand and said, 'I'll be the way you want me to be. A teacher?'

She wiped her eyes with the end of her black veil and said, 'God give you and your brothers happiness and peace.'

I looked for Tal'at and found him mending his old bicycle. That thing was just for mending, not riding. Poor Tal'at.

'Tal'at, Mummy's started smiling again,' I said.

He tried to fix the chain around the pedal-wheel but couldn't. 'Good for you, Eman.'

'You're older than me and you're a man. Maybe you know what happens when a person dies.'

'He goes to heaven. That's what my mother told me.'

'So now Amal is in heaven.'

'Yes, a bird in heaven because she's a baby.'

'Do you think she's happy up there?'

'I would be if I was a bird.'

'Yes . . . and people who go to prison. Do they ever come back?'

He hit the pedal and it rotated. 'Mmm . . . they come back.'

They put out the fire and threw themselves on the ground. Shadeed crawled to the cave's mouth. Flickers of light made their faces look like a horror fantasy: as if they were cold corpses trying to behave like living people. Adnan seemed composed, but Samir started shaking. 'We'll never get out of this shithole alive. Fuck it, Shadeed. Why not surrender?'

'Remember the Movement's charter.'

'To hell with the Movement.'

He raised his head, determined to fight to the last drop of blood. All the tactics he had read about evaporated from his head. Giap? Minh? Che? Shit. He wished then that he had had a proper Fedayeen training in one of the camps in the Arab countries. Try to concentrate, man. He had a glimpse of the scene outside. The file of masked soldiers must be two platoons of infantry. Three helicopters? Tanks? Bloody hell, they were fighting a losing battle. The weapons of the IDF he could make out in the intermittent light of the flare bombs ranged from M-14s to M-74s, rockets, grenades. 'Spread out,' he shouted at his brothers. The noises mingled in his ears: dogs barking, loud-speakers blaring, helicopters hovering, the hissing and coughing of radios. 'Roger. 30 out.' '50 out.' 'Point – ease – FIRE!' A round of machine-gun fire burst into the cave. He slid his body against the ground. He had made up his mind: he would die for Palestine. The crippling fear seeped out of his joints and his body became lighter. He fired back. Samir tried to sit down. 'Lie down, you fool. FLAT!" The bastards were damn close and armed with all the M's in the book. Fuck the Americans. They were completely encircled. He heard the dull sound of marching boots. Samir fired at them until he had finished his ammunition. A heavy burst of automatic fire shook the cave. Some of the bullets stuck in the damp walls and others fell to the ground, digging a grave to bury themselves since they had failed to bury others. He could actually hear the heavy breathing of an Israeli soldier. Were they that bloody close? It must be his imagination.

'Two minutes to surrender,' the loud-speaker barked. Sweat gathered at the tip of his nose, then dropped to the ground. Another round of a different kind of fire. Just one hand grenade tossed in that den and they would all be stories of the past. Adnan was splashed with a liquid of some sort. 'Hell. What's this sticky stuff?' Seconds later the liquid exploded, tearing him into pieces. The earth objected by quivering violently. He couldn't see properly because of the smoke and soot. Better not to see. The same stink as that morning. Human flesh and hair being burnt. Adnan's charred skin melted, leaving a thin coating on the whitish bones. The kneecaps, skull and teeth gleamed in the blazing flames. The drawn lips uttered a gasp, then the corpse quivered. Time had slowed down its pace. He wiped his tears. Inflict the heaviest casualties. He snatched Adnan's Galilee and emptied the damn thing, shooting in every direction. Kill. Kill.

'I can't breathe,' Samir rasped. Another blast: Samir was hit. 'I want to go alone,' he whispered and lurched to the other end of the cave. They had blown tough Samir into shreds of stained rags. Nothing of the 'man' was left to become younger. He should have said freeze man's age or stop him from growing. He was talking to himself in a loud voice. Actually he was screaming. Was he going mad? Adnan's corpse, if he could call that charred skeleton a corpse, clenched as if trying to hold on to the earth. They had reduced Samir the tiger to a few remnants that oozed with blood. His leg was cut in an ugly way. Done by a crazy surgeon in one of his fits. His boot was still on. Shadeed kissed the leg and wondered how trivial things can outlive man, the tiger. He also kissed the forehead bone which used to be the best feature of Adnan's baby-face.

The walls closed in upon him. No ammunition. He held his head high and staggered out of death's den. The sharp stink followed him. Fight and live to fight another day. Fight and live to fight another day. An echo in his skull. The scalding flames were wiped out by the blue sky of Nablus. He wished that he could have a last glimpse of the city sitting in the valley's lap, but the soldiers, a human loop from which hung every kind of death-dealer, blocked his view.

In the night of 9 June 1984, as part of a special intelligence operation conducted by the 4th IDF C-7 section under Major Shlomo Ettan, troops under Lieutenant Yitshak Friedman surrounded a hiding place in Al-Nar mountain, Nablus. The operation was carried out successfully. Two terrorists were killed and the third gave himself up. Intelligence reports confirm that the three terrorists were responsible for the assault in Hebron, as a result of which nine of the Settlers' Committee were killed including the secretary of Kach movement. The new US anti-guerilla weapon was tested for the first time and proved to be very effective. One of our soldiers was slightly injured. The terrorist was taken to Beer Sheva prison.

SECRET – SECRET – SECRET – SECRET –

Mummy told me that Daddy spent most of his time in prison reading verses of the Holy Qur'an, especially 'The Expansion'. I was curious, so I pulled one of the big Qur'ans from the shelf. I sat on the floor and placed the heavy book on my lap. Imitating Daddy, I read the verses loudly:

'In the name of Allah, the Beneficent, the Merciful, "Have we not expanded for you your breast, And taken off from you your burden, Which pressed heavily upon your back, And exalted for you your enemies? Surely with difficulty is ease. With difficulty is surely ease. So when you are free, strive hard, And make your Lord your exclusive object."'

'Mummy, what does "expansion" mean?'

'This chapter was sent to comfort our Prophet. God expanded his breast, which means opened it for the truth. Also, it indicates that his difficulties were not meant to continue.'

'And what does "exclusive", mean?'

'It means "only".'

'Daddy wants to make God his only object, then.'

'Yes, dear.'

'What about me?'

'You come second.'

Daddy was praying to God all the time. I was sure he was unhappy, because the verse said, 'Surely with

difficulty is ease.' He was asking God for 'ease'.
'O God, please help Daddy and give him "ease".'

Shadeed was handcuffed and thrown inside a jeep like a garbage bag. 'Done, sir,' a soldier said enthusiastically. The convoy slid down the mountainside. When the driver started the engine, the metal floor beneath him shuddered. Because they had twisted his hands behind his back, he had to press his cheek on the filth between the black boots of the soldiers sitting on the benches on both sides of the jeep. What would they do to him? Remember, no mercy at all.

'You son of a bitch. You mother-fucker. How dare you kill Israeli citizens?' one of the soldiers said in his funny Arabic.

He pretended that he couldn't hear him and shut his eyes firmly.

'I'd like to split his head with this M-14,' he added and tapped his rifle butt.

He remained calm. Show them that you're not scared. His head flopped like a water-melon by the soldiers' feet. What if he were to shoot?

'Nobody would blame me for that. He's nothing.' They switched to Hebrew. His friend tried to rationalize with him.

'Hey, man. You're wrong. Shin Beit would rip your head off,'

'But he's just an Arab, a terrorist.'

One of them would eventually convince the other,

so by the end of that journey he would be either dead or alive. As if he cared. He wanted to join his brothers. The charred skeleton clenching the ground. Pleading with another force. He wished that they would kill him but he didn't know why he felt like shielding his head with his arms. It was better to die. They would peel his muscles off one by one. He must close his mouth. Everything that was said and done before him should be kept strictly in his own mind. Stop the flow between the brain and the tongue. Uncle Ho, when they cut him into pieces, he wouldn't even have a mouth to keep shut. His sweat dripped to the floor and got mixed with the filth. The reek was unbearable. His? The filth? Nothing like the smell of burnt human flesh. Decomposed fish with rotten egg. He was sure that Adnan would see his daughter. No more. No more. He stuck his forehead to the dirt. That should be his place. Why not surrender, the tiger asked. Shit. Bitterness gushed through his chest to his mouth. Cool it. Must not cry like a woman. Who told them about their hiding place? As long as there was a Palestinian informer, they would never free their country. His mother must be waiting for him. Eman. He missed her so much. Licked by desire, he slid his belly and thighs on the cold metal. He was lost, finished, past tense. He lost control of his joints, his world.

The trip had ended. The serious welcome would start soon. Where in hell was he? The soldiers who had wanted to split his head kicked him flying out of the jeep. Pain and he would be comrades. He staggered to his feet. The sun was coming out coyly, but he was sure that it would grow into a reckless tramp by mid-day. They had brought him to Beer Al-Sab'a Prison? Enter = dead, leave = born. The police station of the British, the prison of the Zionists and the administrative centre of the Ottomans. Fuck the Ottomans, the British and the Zionists! The dry cold pierced into his bones. The desert – like him – always went to the extreme. His jumper was soaked with sweat and his hair stuck to his skull. He stood blindly in front of the prison gate as if struck by a rifle butt on the head. 'Move, move.' That old building would swallow him. A flash of fire. The soldier slapped his face. He blinked. Blood gathered at the corner of his mouth and trickled down. When a drop of his blood hit the ground, the desert soil absorbed it immediately, leaving behind a shadow of red.

A violent push. He tumbled into a dark room. Through the small window near the ceiling, a faint light squeezed itself. The stink of blood, sweat and urine hit his face. The nightmare had started and would never end. Of course, he was dreaming. They hadn't taken him to prison and blown his brothers up. Rusty metal grated together. The heavy door moved into place. The beat of his heart sounded like an African drum hit by tropical boughs. Fear crippled him and pinned his limbs to the floor.

'What's your name?'

He shuddered because he couldn't see the ghost talking to him. A spotlight was suddenly put on and pointed at the centre of his eyes. Patches of light in all colours – then total blindness. He sensed the presence of other people in the room. A trail of smoke. Someone was smoking in the room. The light was switched off. Some colourful patches. Two fat legs. A blond soldier with a beer belly and blue gleaming eyes stared at him. His chin moved rapidly trying to squeeze the slippery chewing gum.

'What's your name? I said, what's your name? David, give him a treat,' said the voice wearily.

David started beating him up with his cudgel. When he got the first blow he didn't feel anything, but seconds later a flash of fire burnt his body. He flinched, winced, then began shivering. Fuck them.

'What's your name?'

'Shadeed,' he wheezed. Must think of other things. Recite poetry. Toufiq Ziad.

> Here, on your chests, we are staying like a wall
> Starving, naked, challenging
> Reciting poems
> Filling the angry streets with demonstrations
> Filling the prisons with dignity
> Making children a vengeful generation . . .
> After generation . . .

The words flew away in the horizon like pigeons. What's-your-name-and-cudgel went on and on until he heard the splash of water in their fountain. The scent of citrus plantation and flowers and herbs of their indoor garden filled his nostrils. Thyme and citrus. The floor of the yard was always cool. The drizzle of the fountain. Jaffa. The fishermen played the lute and sang on the beach:

> Why sea? Why?
> You are laughing and
> My tears are flowing.

Cold water engulfed him. Shit, he was drowning. The water dashed into his ears. He shivered and pushed his body upwards to keep floating. His wet body was still burning with pain.

'What's your name?'

'Shadeed.'

'No, leave him. Say, "Shadeed, my master".'

47

'Shadeed,' he moaned.

David flogged him with his whip. His mushed flesh couldn't take the pressure of a feather, let alone that carving edge. His skull exploded and he screamed, 'Shadeed, my master.'

'Good boy. Well-mannered. What's your father's name?'

'Mahmud, my master.'

'Family?'

'Al-Falastini, my master.' Trivial. Blood. Charred corpses.

'You're Palestinian, then. Beat him.'

David raised his strong arm and hit him. The sharp edge flayed his skin. When he saw the whip encircling his waist, he shouted hysterically, 'A snake. A snake, my master.'

'Yes, a snake. Of course. Your birthplace?'

He was exhausted and wanted to go to sleep. Let him be. Enough. Soot. He pulled his lips with difficulty and whispered, 'Nablus.' The sparrows twittered in his heart.

'Birth date?'

'1/4/1964.'

'Heh heh, right at the very beginning.'

He used to insert his hand in the wild pigeon's nest looking for eggs. Once, a rattlesnake shook its bells and he knew that it was lurking inside. He ran as fast as he could, but the rattle followed him.

'They started the proceedings in the Military Court yesterday,' said Mummy, looking at her fingers.

'Well of course, they have the confessions, they need to start a show trial,' my Aunt Hanin said heatedly.

'They tortured them severely. I know that, although your brother hasn't told me a thing.'

'What do you expect? My brother is a member of the National Freedom Party. He tried a coup d'état with the help of the army. We wanted to found a democratic state – we already have one of the bloody things – what do you think they'll give him for all that rubbish? A kiss?'

'We need a good lawyer, but that will cost us a fortune.'

'We'll sell all our jewellery. I don't need mine any more. Who cares about wearing golden bracelets? The whole world is collapsing. I don't have to look beautiful to die.'

'God forbid. You're still young.'

'Young? Me? I'm an old spinster . . . anyway, forget about me now. What about money?'

They were drinking black coffee in the kitchen. 'Money' seemed to be very important. I decided to stop taking the two piasters. I talked and played with no one at school. During the break I used to eat and drink nothing. Going there without money would make no difference. I didn't need money. 'Mummy, I don't need my pocket-money,' I said. I thought that she would be relieved, but instead she looked sad and hurt.

My uncle bought us some apples. I waited for mine. 'Eman, it's your turn. Have one, dear,' Mummy said. I didn't know why I felt like crying. My eyes and my nose were running most of the time. Tal'at was annoyed with me. He said I looked messy and dirty. Like the beggar who used to come to our neighbourhood with his mother, Um-Bsys. Her house was on the top of the high mountain I could see out of our window. Whenever Um-Bsys visited our area, all the children disappeared, including me of course.

'Why don't you comb your hair, or wash your face. You look ugly,' said Tal'at.

'It's because of Mummy. She's stopped buying me pretty ribbons. She hardly looks at our faces nowadays.'

'What do you think? You're a big family. Eman, since you're the eldest, why not help? Try to do something around the house. You can't stay a spoilt child forever.'

'Tal'at, I am not a spoiled child. I miss Daddy, Tal'at. I want him back.'

That night I couldn't sleep for thinking of Daddy and Tal'at's words. He was right. It was high time for me to help Mummy. The next morning, I washed the dishes. It was not easy. I had to stand on a chair to reach the sink. When I finished, Mummy looked at me and smiled. 'Eman, you're not going to school today. We'll visit one of our relatives.'

'Yes, Mummy.'

'Uncle Amin. Do you remember him?'

'No, Mummy.'

The Democratic State of Israel – Beer Sheva – 1984

The first glimpse David had of the terrorist he had
read so much about in the papers was when a soldier
threw him handcuffed out of the jeep that chilly
morning. He was a dark, average man. A typical
Arab. His eyes were close to each other like a fox's.
The bastard looked exhausted and frightened, which
would definitely make his job easier. He would drag
a confession from these dry lips in three days. Might
as well teach him something about life and people.
He rubbed his arm. So bloody cold. He would never
get used to that weather. In the Agency's leaflets,
Beer Sheva had seemed sunny and warm. He would
finish his shift that day at five. 'Move, move,' he
shouted at the bastard. Didn't he hear him? He was
familiar with the initial shock the prisoners suffered
when they first saw that door. He would soon get
used to the dampness like a mole. At home under the
ground, in the darkness. He wanted to give him just a
sample of his talent, so he slapped him as hard as he
could. Stupid, lazy Arabs. Bare feet. Bare minds.
They don't grasp whatever you tell them. How many
things did the Jews have to teach these grinning
Arabs, he wondered.

He pushed him inside, eager to start working on
him. Cut him into size. When would that flood of
arrogant fools stop? He had been working in this

stinking prison for fifteen long years. Growing old, David? He started beating the terrorist up when the officer told him to. Teach the bastard how to behave in the future, if he had a future. He did his job mechanically because he knew by heart where to hit to cause the most intense pain. It came with experience. When he was a green soldier, the idea of inflicting pain had terrified him, then he got used to it. He liked to do a clean job and watch the colour of the prisoner's skin change from red-crimson-purple to indigo. When the left side of the body became a mixture of black and purple he would switch to the right. The ultimate was an even colour all over. Even Mokady couldn't do better. He created a new image out of the natural elements available to him. The Open Museum had a lovely collection of sculpture that he wanted to see. But Judith didn't feel like it at present. She was in one of her meditative moods that he couldn't break through.

'SOLDIER. He's unconscious.'

Shit. He was flogging him while he was unconscious. Damn it. He wiped his forehead with his sleeve and sat down to drink his Turkish coffee. No clean spot to put his cup in that dusty room. The fresh flowers and clean roads of Zawichest in Poland flashed in his mind. Tendrils of pink rose trees climbed the white walls of his village. He had tried them in his garden, but the soil was too salty and needed a lot of water before it was purified.

'Splash him with water.'

'Sir.' He brought a bucket of water and poured it on the terrorist's head. He looked like a rat soaked in blood. Give him some of the whip business. The kid began disintegrating. The beginning of the end. He thought that the whip was a real snake. Damn funny, that. They have rotten minds. Thanks to Marx and

52

his lot. Should be dragged down to earth. Equality? Paradise? All bull-shit. The bastard was only twenty years old. Why do they play dangerous games? They blow themselves to pieces because they can't handle explosives. Too young to get mixed up with the RPG kids. He mumbled away to himself, then fainted.

'Enough for today, soldier. Make sure that he's comfortable.'

'Yes, Sir.' While he was doing the hard work, the officer sat on a comfortable chair. David do this. David do that. As if he were his private maid. All his colleagues got promoted except him. The dirty job for him and the clean interrogation for them. He handcuffed the bastard to the window and went back home.

His old Fiat coughed when he started the engine. The sun glowed in the sky and spread a golden layer over the world. Even the stinking prison looked like the palace of dreams. He spat out the chewing-gum, rubbed his tired chin and put on his sunglasses. The disintegrating car barely covered the two miles between his house and the prison. He had bought it from a bastard Arab. Never trust an Arab. Money makes the world go round. If he had enough he would buy a Honda Civic. Metallic smoky-blue. Finesse. He parked the car in front of the garden gate. Garden? Salty grains that made even honey salty. 'The land flowing with milk and honey.' Shit. He opened the gate and went in. He had tried everything in that dump. Nothing grew except the weeds. He looked at the Finberts' garden next door. A huge grapevine rested on a wooden trellis. Green pearls hanging down like lamps. Mordecai, the bastard, had a decent garden. The holes that looked like mole burrows made his failure visible. He held the shovel and tried to flatten the ground to its former

53

shape. He raised his hand and hit. The frightened eyes of the terrorist were mingled with the soil. Pleading? Begging? When he raised his arm again he saw Mordecai watching him across the fence.

'Good evening, David,' he said coldly. The Bible was in his hand as usual. Reading holy books, holy Mordecai.

'Good evening.'

'A good day?' he asked in a toneless voice. David knew that he didn't approve of his job.

'Yes, my friend.'

Mordecai shook his skullcapped head and disappeared behind a giant pine tree. The pathetic vine was the only thing that survived in his garden. He threw down the shovel and went inside.

'Have you seen his garden?' he asked Judith.

'Very beautiful,' she said.

'Yes, darling.' Saint Jud was talking again. She didn't belong to the world of mortals like him. Sometimes he wished he could keep his tools at home. He wanted to snip off all the leaves in Mordecai's garden with his whip.

'Dinner, Jud,' he said, imitating the senior officer.

'Ready, darling.'

The Democratic State of Ishmael – Rahmah – 1969

I put on my best dress. It was printed with pink roses.
Unfortunately, the hem was stained with dry mud. I
tried to shake it off. Mummy was wearing her black
dress and covered her head with her black veil. We
took a taxi. 'Nahar, please,' Mummy said to the
driver.

He moved his greasy head and said, 'At your
service.' His mirror sunglasses reflected the crowded
street. The interior of the car was decorated with
stickers of beautiful women, red lights and plastic
roses. 'When you see, say, "In the name of God",'
was written in green on the black tableau. A singer
with a husky voice was singing, 'My love whispered
in my ears. Wash, wash.' The driver took off his
mirror glasses and looked at Mummy in a strange
way. 'Which street?' he asked.

'Liberation Street, please.'

'Do you know the place exactly?'

'No, I don't. I've never been there before. We can
ask.'

The driver moved his eyebrows upwards and
downwards in a funny way and said softly, 'Yes,
beautiful one, we have to keep asking. Haven't we?'

Mummy lowered her eyes. The driver put on his
mirror glasses again and started repeating with the
singer, 'Wash, wash, wash, wash.'

We arrived at Uncle Amin's house. It was a very clean area. In front of the big house there was a spacious garden full of pink roses like the ones on my dress. We climbed the stairs and Mummy rang the bell. It gave out a lovely tune. Mummy rubbed her hands together, then pressed the button again. A woman wearing a black dress, white cap and white apron opened the door. 'God help you,' she said and slammed the door.

Mummy rang the bell again. 'I am not a beggar. I want to see Mr. Amin Saqi. I am his brother's wife.' The woman ran her eyes over us disapprovingly and said, 'Wait outside.'

We waited and waited in front of that door. My knees started shaking, so we sat down on the steps. They were sparkling. I began comparing the stained roses of my dress with the real ones of the garden. The real ones had a very nice smell like Mummy's perfume. She used to wear it in the past. I'd have loved to live in a place like this. Big windows, trees, flowers. I saw myself wearing a diamond crown and descending the stairs like the Queen. I saw her picture in the newspaper. She was wearing a long velvet cloak and a shining dress. Her Majesty Queen Elizabeth. I had a dark-blue velvet ribbon. Daddy bought it for me before he went to prison. I could wear it in the festival, he said. I felt sorry for Lulu so I gave it to her as a present. She tied it around her waist to hide her wound.

'You can come in now. But please take off your shoes first.' Mummy looked at me, squeezed my hand, and then started taking off her shoes. I took mine off very quickly because the buckle was broken. We entered the house. No. No. Paradise. I could see nothing but turquoise and gold. Ash-trays, roses, lamps, all in turquoise and gold, were displayed on glass shelves. I stood there looking at that huge room. Was this Alice's wonderland? Ali-Baba's cave? No. No. The giant's palace. I was waiting for El-Shatter Hassen to appear when Mummy pulled my hand. We went into another magnificent sitting room.

An elderly man was sitting on the sofa. 'Good afternoon, girl,' he said to me. I stepped back. How dare he call me 'girl'? Mummy sat down and said, 'How are you, my brother?'

'Fine. Fine. How are you, Um-Eman?'

'God help us, my brother. They'll start the court proceedings soon. We should hire a good lawyer as soon as possible.'

'We?'

Mummy rubbed her trembling hands together. 'Yes, we. Could you lend us some money? Your brother is in danger.'

'He used to be my brother. Not after what he did.'

'He *is* your brother.'

'He showed me up. Humiliated me. How dare he put his head next to the ruler's? Ridiculous.'

'I'll return the money as soon as they release him.'

'What he did – no, what he tried to do – affected my business. Nobody wants to make deals with the traitor's brother, of course.'

'Please, help us.'

'No, I'll not stick my fingers into this case.'

Mummy stood up and then sat down. She said, 'God protect your children. Please help us. He's in serious danger now. They might hang him. What will happen to his four children if he dies?' Mummy's tears ran down her cheeks. She wiped them with the end of her black veil.

He waved his hand saying, 'Girl, come here. Take this piaster.'

How dare he call me 'girl'? I stepped back.

'I am sorry, I can't help you though my heart is with you.'

'Oh, can't you?' shouted Mummy. 'Eman, come on, let's go. There's no place here for people like us.'

When we left the big house, the sun was setting. 'We'll walk to the bus-stop.'

'They have buses like us?'

'Yes, dear, for the servants to go home.'

'Mummy, why don't we live in a place like this? At least I could play in the garden with Tal'at.'

'Because few people can afford it. We would have to be rich to live here.'

For the first time in my life I realized that we were poor. I was poor? Fragments of incidents, places and people started to some together. Because we were poor, we didn't have a garden, a big house and a clean neighbourhood. Because we were poor, Amal died and Lulu was killed. Most probably, Daddy did what he did because we were poor.

We took the bus to the eastern part of Rahmah. The nearer we were to the other side of the city, the dirtier the streets and people. Even the smell of the air changed. We started with the odour of roses and ended up with the stink of over-flowing sewage systems. Half-naked children were playing with their shit. 'Why are they doing that?'

'Because they have no toys.'

It was dark when we arrived. The once spacious road shrank to a narrow alley. Our jasmine tree was standing alone near the verandah. Filth could be seen everywhere. I wanted to be Alice or the Queen.

Occupied Palestine – Beer Al-Sab'a – 1984

David suspended Shadeed from the window bars by his handcuffs. 'I wish you a very good night,' he said and went out of the room closing the heavy door behind him. The muscles of his hands and shoulders ached. He couldn't take any more. Every now and then the tormenting silence was broken with an echo of a moan. He was swept by joy when he heard the first moan. He was not alone. He felt better. The moans were like the sounds of wounded animals which had no connection with this world. Darkness and piercing cold. He couldn't make out any of his surroundings. He shivered when he remembered the iron cudgel which was stained with his own blood. They deserted him, left him alone swinging between earth and sky. No gravity, just non-stop floating. Eman blushed when he kissed her. Sad, lovely eyes. Adnan's blurred baby-face. Why did Adnan leave him alone swinging like a pendulum? Why did he go? Slod. Slod. Slod. Time passed behind his back, outside in that desert. Every passing second was a giant trudging in sticky slush. He wanted to switch his mind off and go to sleep, to stretch his arms and catch that floating ball and stick it to his neck again. Why didn't they kill him? Slod. Slod. Slod. A thin moan. His head drooped.

Just seconds later, he heard David's voice, 'Shalom.'

Peace? It couldn't be imported. It would never spread over their country until these aggressors stopped polluting their air. David unlocked the handcuffs. 'Let's give our baby a break.' He fell down to the ground.

'Take off your clothes,' he said excitedly. Shadeed opened his mouth.

'Take off your clothes.' He looked at them stupidly. David kicked him and shouted, 'Move.' It came home to him that he must strip himself. He fumbled with the buttons of his trousers, which resisted the beating bravely. He took them off. 'Go on.' His upbringing paralysed his hands. The officer grew impatient and belted him with his fist. He bent his body, winded. When he raised his head, he saw clearly the ragged faces of his jailers. He slipped off his pants. Standing stark naked between them, he felt so defenceless. Totally at their mercy. Just like an animal trapped by a group of bitter hunters. Bones and flesh against them and their tools. His legs became so limp that they couldn't carry him. He tried to steady himself.

'Shadeed Mahmud Al-Falastini, where do you live?'

'In Nablus, my master.'

'Where in bloody Nablus?'

'In Tel Al-Asaker refugee camp, my master.'

'You went to an UNRWA school?'

'Yes, my master, and ate UNRWA food since I was born.'

'I don't think the UNRWA fed you your progressive ideas. . .'

'. . .'

'Look, Shadeed, you're still young. You have a good future in front of you. Why waste yourself? Do you think the Movement gives a damn about you?

60

They should have prepared a better plan. If they did you wouldn't have lost your brothers, Samir and Adnan.'

'Adnan . . . Samir. How are they? Are they still alive?'

'They're fine. Perfect.'

'I want to see them.'

'You will. Look, Shadeed, even the head of your Movement met our oficials last month in Japan. Can't you see? Can't you see who pays and who gets the profit? Be sensible, my boy. All I want from you, young man, is one piece of information. Who gave you the Galilee machine-guns? It's very simple. Think about the happy years to come. You'll be released. You'll be a free man living peacefully with your woman. Your sweetheart. Her name is Eman. Isn't it? Don't you love her?'

Sad eyes. Sad eyes, he wished she could see what they did to him. Never give up. Confuse them. Say anything.

'David, break his silence.'

Would they start peeling his muscles? Nothing much left of them. He started shaking.

David smiled and said, 'Fuck you, woman. You're trembling.'

One morning, I was sewing a cloak for Lulu. Tal'at came and said, 'What are you doing? Sewing again. Let's go outside and play together.'

It was windy that day. Rida and all the boys of the neighbourhood were there. We started playing 'Liala'. In each game we had to choose a beautiful one. That day we picked Rida. She sat in the middle of the circle, smiling. She was blonde with a milk-white skin. Her red dress was printed with white circles. A good choice on our part. She was very pretty.

We grew tired of that game, so we decided to cook petals in empty cans. We wanted to light a fire, so we asked Rida to bring a box of matches. She stole one from their kitchen and came running. When we set fire to some papers, the fire caught Rida's dress. She started shouting. Within seconds, she had become a ball of flames. I dropped the can and rushed to tell Mummy what had happened. 'Mummy, Mummy, Rida!' I shouted. She couldn't hear me. I started crying and pleading, 'Rida, Rida.'

I couldn't sleep for three nights. Rida's image in fire was planted in my eyes. I tried to shut my ears with my fingers. No use. Her cries were ringing inside me. 'Eman, Eman, Uh, Uh.' They told me that Rida had been taken to hospital and that I couldn't see her. Not for a while at least. But I heard my aunt Hanin saying to Mummy, 'They cut two of her ribs. She's in the ICU. They're not sure if she'll stay alive.' Grown-ups never tell the truth. I needed explanations and support badly, but received none.

I lost the people I loved, one by one. First, Lulu was killed. Second, Daddy was taken away, though they said he would come back. Third, my little sister, Amal. Fourth, Rida. Fifth, Mummy, who became a different person. She had drifted away from me lately. I wiped my tears and said, 'Oh God, from now on I'll never love anyone. I don't want my loved ones to suffer. Forgive me, God, for loving them and making them suffer.'

That morning, David noticed that the oozing terrorist was well-done. He preferred his steak that way. With some vinegar and baked potato. Mmm. When he touched the potato with his knife, the skin peeled very smoothly.

'Take off your clothes.'

Eh, he had forgotten that the Arab's culture was one of totem and taboo. The bastard refused to move his hands and show them his treasures. Mohammad told him that even when they made love to their wives they kept their clothes on. Damn funny thing, that. It was his weakest spot. Must play that tune more often. He just couldn't do it. Marvellous! 'Go on.' His favourite game was peeling. He loved helping Jud in the kitchen cleaning and cutting vegetables.

The UNRWA. They were really the ones who pampered those kids. The UNRWA was responsible for the survival of Palestinian refugees. The result: the RPG kids. With their powdered milk, they watered herbs that should be weeded out. He remembered the dump called his garden and started beating him up with a renewed anger. The government promised more water. God only knows when. He had green fingers, but his major problem was lack of water.

'Soldier, the prisoner believes that he is a hero. Break his silence. You don't concentrate enough.'

'Yes, sir,'

'After three days, physical torture is pointless.'

The officer was talking as if he knew everything about David's job. David had taught him the phrase he'd just used! Their part was ridiculously simple. They repeated the same questions over and over again. Once, one of them had asked him to hit the prisoner on the head. Of course, he refused to obey the command. He inflicted pain but never to the extent of making one of his cases deformed or mad. In his deceptively easy job, there were fine limits between the possible and the forbidden. He was quite experienced. Because of that, he could see the limits. He hit artistically to cause the least harm and the most pain. Without him in that room they would never get a tiny piece of information. Later, they would blame him if the prisoner didn't confess. It collapsed on the head of the weakest. He might as well kiss good-bye to the promotion and the 20,000 shekels he was waiting for. No metallic Honda Civic. The dull ache in his head developed into the usual migraine. It was getting worse every passing day. Either him or that prisoner in that room. The prisoner was scared, so it seemed to him that was the right moment to insult him.

'Fuck you, woman. You're trembling,' he said and went on beating him up. He fainted again. Shit. He'd wasted his last chance.

Twenty years old? Young and silent. He'd never encountered such courage in his whole career. The terrorist had curled himself up on the floor like a worm.

'Fine. Transfer him to X-Section. I am sick of it,' said the officer. He signed a piece of paper and left the room in a hurry.

David looked at the terrorist for the first time. His name was Shadeed? Some of his thick hair had fallen out, showing a peeling skull. His thin body was an even purple in colour. The clear eyes had lost their sparkle and had become yellowish and dry. His cheek bones stretched his skin like tent poles. Keeping his mouth open, his jaw moved up and down. He licked his upper lip with a white tongue. Shit, his left arm was broken. When? He wanted to know when. He threw the whip on the floor, spat out the chewing-gum and clumped out of the stinking room.

PART TWO

The Democratic State of Ishmael – Rahmah – 1977

Thanks to Habub's rattling bus, all the people of the neighbourhood turned out to watch the trial. After squeezing themselves out of the decaying vehicle, the group stood bewildered in a spacious yard in front of a huge building. Five wide steps led to a platform full of tall columns which supported the grey structure. The high walls were covered with a thick blackish layer deposited patiently by years and pollution. The pillars were lined as if a spider had been weaving its threads around them for centuries. To let us in, the guards moved a huge chain off a hook. 'What is this?' asked Abdu, the baker. He was accompanied as usual by his Egyptian 'boy', Sheiha. 'Cheap Egyptians. I give him just 20 dinars and he sweeps the bakery floor with his eyelashes,' Abdu used to say. The laundryman, Ghazzaleh, was wearing a tight white shirt and black trousers. He came to see his best customer creased. Abu-Ibrahim, the grocer, was wearing his army uniform, but for the sake of formalities he added a green tie. He had been dismissed from the army after claiming that he was deaf. He looked remote, pushing a stone backwards and forwards with his foot.

Smoking a slim cigarette, Yassin walked briskly around the group. Being the only, but the best, barber in the area, he had lived up to his reputation by re-arranging his hair for the occasion. It was thin, and glistened with grease. He kept running his fingers over his head, which was waved in the 20's Freed Al-Attrash style. My mother loved that singer. She used to lull us to sleep with his lines,

'I miss you, I miss you,
And greetings I had sent you.'

Zarour, the coffee cook, with his once white apron, jumped into the bus at the last minute, confirming his belonging to the neighbourhood. The thin chemist was shaking, afraid of the grey spider. All the people of Al-Rabia' neighbourhood were dressed up and wearing thin ties, all ready to see their customer or friend torn to pieces

My aunt, Hanin – that name suited her, she was always nostalgic about something – was eye-catching in her dark-red mini skirt and white blouse. The sleeves were bull-fighter's style, taking away a few inches of her precious height. Her hair had lately turned rusty blonde. She was uncomfortable in high, bulky-heeled sandals. I kept looking at her, afraid that she might lose her balance. The barber's eyes were sneaking to her white legs every now and then. Daddy wouldn't approve.

My mother, pale and exhausted, sat down on the ground. I sat next to her. Um-Musaad and the old woman who claimed to be my grandmother joined us. They were all wearing black. Lumpy bundles of black. Confused and lost ravens. Why black? He was not dead.

Abdu opened a plastic bag he was carrying, took out some sesame cakes, then gave them to Sheiha to sell. He started crying, 'We have cake, hot and delicious.' Zarour followed suit and started selling coffee out of a stained thermos he was holding. The barber went to Sheiha to buy one. 'Six piasters,' Sheiha said in his funny Ishmaelian accent.

'You bastard. Double?'

'Transportation and other expenses,' said Sheiha, smiling mischievously.

Yassin searched his pockets and handed him a ten-piaster piece. He walked towards my aunt, then stopped, turned left, and went to Zarour. After buying a cup of coffee, he came, hands full, to my aunt. He offered her what he had. She eyed him disgustedly and moved her head to the other direction.

'Please take them before the coffee gets cold.'

'Thank you. I don't want anything from you.'

'Please.'

'All right, I will take them, but please get out of my sight.'

Hanin started chewing the cake and Yassin ran his hand over his shining head and smiled, not forgetting of course to pay homage to the white legs.

My aunt wanted to get married to a rich man and for love, but imprisoned in Al-Rabia' neighbourhood, breaking through was not going to be easy. Once she had visited her brother Amin. Right away his wife accused her of stealing a crystal cup . . . Yassin's neck was beginning to hurt, because he kept looking downwards, then upwards with a jerk.

The sun was getting hotter. Everybody was eating, drinking and chatting except the three ravens, Abu-Ibrahim and me. I was surprised to hear a bird singing. There were no trees around. How come a bird was living there? I remembered Tal'at. I wished that he were there. His eyes were full of tears when he left.

Tal'at's eyes were shining in the sunshine. He was suppressing his tears. Men do not cry. His white shirt was dangling out of the half-closed suitcase. White. Always white flowers, jasmine formed like a necklace. He used to place them around my neck. I used to brush my cheeks with the smooth petals. Their odour filled our bedroom. The next day the jasmine became brown with an unpleasant smell. I liked Tal'at's dark skin. He used to place his hand over mine and say, 'Good God, coffee and milk.'

He said in a shaking voice, 'I am leaving for America. I won't see you for some time, but I will come back. I promise.' They all say that. 'You'll be fine, don't worry,' he added.

'Yes, I will,' I answered in a thin voice.

'Take care. O.K.?'

'I want you to know that I hate you.' I gave him my hand, to pick a finger. He chose the forefinger. He wanted us to stay friends? 'Give me your hand.' He stretched his fingers and I slowly touched his little finger. I would never speak to him again. I ran to our house. It was dark inside. I looked for Lulu and found her on the top of our closet wrapped in a plastic bag used for garbage. It was covered with dust. I unwrapped her and then hugged her. 'Oh, Lulu, Lulu, even Tal'at is leaving.' In the darkness, I could barely see her face. The colour of the edges of her velvet ribbon was fading. 'Lulu, what should I do?'

I remembered when Tal'at first told me that he was leaving. I was sitting next to him while he was drawing the map of the Arab World for me. 'The Arab World extends from the Arab Gulf to the Pacific Ocean,' the teacher used to say. 'Our mountains are high, our valleys are deep, our plains are green, our past is glorious . . . Tra-la-la, Tra-la-la.' I used to colour maps by scratching the paper with a pencil. Tal'at was patient. He used to chop the head of the pencil very gently with a blade, making small bits of colour. Then, he put the brown bits over the mountains and rubbed them with a piece of cotton. The result was a puff of colour, hazy, even and light. I used to watch the magical process, breathless. When Tal'at finished the map he looked at me and said, 'Here you are.'

'It is beautiful. I will get 100 out of 100. Thank you.'

'Eman, control your temper. I want to tell you something.'

'Go ahead. Tell me.'

'I will leave for America next month.'

'Why?' I asked, utterly confused.

'It is better for my future.'

'I don't understand.'

'You will when you grow older.'

'Oh, will I?'

I snatched the map, scattering the coloured pencils all over the room. I walked out of my best friend's house, then looked at the map. The colours lost their magic. I could see some lines in the even shade. Lines, sketches, pillars and spiders. I was leaning on my mother's shoulder. The sun was in the middle of the sky. All the group was sitting down by then except Hanin. Abdu and Zarour were out of cake and coffee. Abu-Ibrahim was still engrossed in deep sad thoughts.

'Queue up like civilised people,' a bedouin soldier shouted. Everybody stood up startled. They shook off the dust from their clothes. My mother was first in the queue. I was right behind her. Um-Musaad, the old woman, then Hanin. Sticking to Hanin's back was the barber. I looked at the black gate. I hadn't seen Daddy for some time. My heart started beating. All my eagerness and love were reflected in Abu-Ibrahim's eyes.

Two soldiers ordered us to enter. We proceeded sluggishly into a long corridor. Each step brought more darkness, as if I was stepping on buttons and switching off invisible lights. It took me seconds to get used to the dim light. On both sides of the corridor wooden seats were fixed. They were like low shelves. A skeleton-thin woman was sitting on one of the shelves breast-feeding her baby. My sister Amal must have been flying in heaven. One of paradise's birds.

An old man was sitting next to the woman. He was making gestures with his stick and saying incomprehensible words. 'You tyrants, you pagans,' a woman was shouting. A whisper from a soldier shut her up. At the end of the passage four children were sitting on the floor, surrounding their mother. They looked at us with their big eyes. A lady wearing a bright red dress came out of one of the doors. She said in a husky voice, 'Thank you,' then roared with wild laughter. Her face was barely visible under the green and red paint.

The bedouin soldier looked sternly at us and said, 'This way.' We turned right and entered a spacious hall. We took our seats at long desks like the ones in our school. The floor was covered with filth which gave off a bad smell like the government hospital I went to with my mother when she was ill. At the far end of the hall there was a high platform on which stood a huge table. I had never seen anything like it before. 'What is that table for?' I asked my mother in a low voice. 'Ssh.' Beside myself with excitement, I fixed my eyes on the desk in front of me. A sticker, 'With the compliments of Mansour and Sons, your local carpenters,' was glued on the left side.

The windows were covered with dirt, light could not penetrate the brownish panes. It was dark and cold inside. I began to shiver and moved closer to my mother. I was wearing one of her old dresses that had been taken in at the sides to fit my waist. The material was getting thinner and thinner, almost see-through. I wanted velvet, but oh, as they say, 'Lucifer dreaming of heaven.'

'Stand up,' shouted a soldier. We rose clumsily. Three middle-aged men entered the court and took their places right in front of us behind a small desk. Their expressions were composed. Unlike everybody else, they felt at home in that dark, stinking hall. They were wearing black robes with satin edges. Three old judges entered from an invisible door and stood erect behind the huge table. In their black robes, they looked like eagles ready to dive on their prey. A door on the left side opened and two soldiers entered, then Daddy. I couldn't look at his face at first. Then gradually I raised my eyes towards the box. He was wearing the same white robe. His iron-grey hair framed his colourless face. Ignoring us, he focused his eyes on a faraway spot. He walked lamely towards the wooden seat in the defendant's box. A muscle in his right cheek was quivering. God give him 'ease'.

The judge in the middle sat down. 'Sit down.' We took our seats. All the people in black started fumbling with papers. I couldn't help it – I pushed my mother and ran towards the platform. I caught the end of the judge's robe with my hand and said to him with a shaking voice, 'I don't love Daddy. Believe me, I don't love him.' My throat began to swell up until flames exploded in front of my eyes. I saw Rida, Amal, Tal'at . . . I sobbed out the same words again and again until the soldier took me by the back of my dress and threw me into my place. Through tears and snot, I looked at Daddy. A faint smile showed on his pale face. He looked like the old man who was gesturing with his stick in the corridor outside.

I wiped my tears and blew my nose with my handkerchief. It was dirty. It used to be yellow, but then, like anything else in that court, it became grey. My ears were hurting with the deep silence. The judge took off his glasses and addressed one of the middle-aged men saying, 'the prosecution'. The man rose to his feet enthusiastically. He straightened his back, grasped the edges of his robe and started a long speech. The words coming out of his mouth were full and ringing as if he gargled with them first, then splashed them at us.

'Ladies and gentlemen, we are here today to pass a verdict on the traitor Mahmud Saqi. What did he do? In 1969, this very man standing in front of you tried to overthrow the government. Some call it a coup d'état. Some even call it a revolution. I call it, sirs, high treason. As the second man in the banned National Freedom Party, it was possible for him to plan the takeover of the main arms of the state, especially the armed forces. They infiltrated the army, picked some key individuals, and neutralized or converted them. This very man went to Derek army camp five times in one month. Seven visits to Einneh. Why? What on earth had the owner of a cheap bookshop to do with army bases?'

He cleared his throat and looked at my aunt in a strange way, then continued, 'Look at his poor family sitting there. What an irresponsible person he is! Look at his poor sister . . .'

The judge interrupted the prosecutor's speech with his hammer. 'You are digressing,' he said angrily.

The prosecutor stretched his arms, making sure that

his robe would spread like huge wings, and said, 'God will not forgive them, the ruler and our country. They are the scum of our clean society. Your honour, you should throw away all the pity in your heart when you deal with them.'

The judge took off his glasses and said, 'Yes, next time. Today, I have an important meeting with someone from the palace. Court dismissed,' he shouted and knocked his hammer.

Daddy was still staring at that spot. He turned his head towards us, then disappeared inside.

'Let's go,' my mother said desperately.

'Where's the bloody lawyer I hired? I'll wrench his head off,' said Um-Musaad. She was furious.

'This man will make it hard for us,' my mother said.

'He's good-looking,' said Hanin.

'Oh, Hanin, why don't you shut up,' barked Um-Musaad.

We gathered in the yard and waited for Habub to show up. The prosecutor tapped on Hanin's shoulder and said, 'I want to talk to you'. She looked at my mother quizzically. My mother nodded her head. They went into the building together.

'Why did you let her go with that wolf?' asked Um-Musaad.

'He might tell her something about the case.'

Um Musaad shook her head and said, 'My sister, who bothers about dancers in the dark.'

When she joined us, Hanin's face was as red as a tomato.

'What does he want?' asked Um-Musaad.

'Nothing really,' said Hanin, 'he wanted to know if I . . . we were managing without my brother.'

'The wolf has a heart after all,' said Um-Musaad thoughtfully.

David kissed Judith on her cheek and said, 'Hello, dear.'

'Hello, love.' She rubbed his shoulder with her hand and asked, 'Exhausting day?'

'Very. We transferred the terrorist to X-Section. I couldn't break his silence.'

'Please David, I don't want to hear about it,' she said decidedly. 'Will you give me a hand, love?'

'Yes, I'll wash my hands first.'

David looked at his reflection in the mirror. Some grey had crept into his hair. He was annoyed. Life slipped through his fingers like water. He hadn't even got that bloody promotion. A comfortable chair plus an electric fan in that suffocating heat which made his underarms and spine wet. He put on a clean cotton T-shirt and looked at his reflection again. He was developing a beer-belly.

Stop drinking beer and stick to wine. He walked lightly to the kitchen, opened the freezer, took out a misty beer can, then opened the can and sipped the icy liquid. The refreshing cold drink ran down his throat. He felt better.

'What do you want me to do?'

'Can you cut the carrots for me?'

He took a knife from the drawer and started cleaning, then cutting the carrots into almost identical slices. 'Jud, how was your day?'

'Nothing exciting. The kids behaved themselves today.'

'Good.'

'No, I really love it when they fill the place with their noise.'

David looked at Judith's belly. She was in good shape. Her narrow waist reminded him of the dry land of Beer Sheva. No fruit at all. After all these years, he still could not believe that he couldn't make that waist more rounded. He needed a son badly. A noisy little creature who would fill the void in his chest. Their country needed hands. Was he really sterile? Should he see the doctor again? David wiped the sweat from his forehead, picked up the can and rushed out of the steaming kitchen.

'David, David,' Judith called and ran after him leaving the pot on the cooker. 'What's wrong, love?'

'Nothing'.

'Please, what is it? You look so upset'

He shrugged his shoulders and said, 'Nothing really, but I want to see the doctor again.'

'Oh, no, please love, why go through it again? I'm happy with you as you are.' She touched his shoulder and asked, 'Have I said something wrong?'

David touched her cheek gently with his fingers and said, 'No, Jud. You see, today I realized that if we had had a son as soon as we got married, he would be twenty years old.' His eyes were gleaming when he added in a choked voice, 'A young chap.'

Judith hugged him and ran her hands across his stiff back. 'Yes,' she whispered, nodding.

David tossed his head from one side to another. His naked body glistened under the dim light of the table lamp. It was trembling. He started moaning and pushing fiercely. He raised his arms protectively. 'No.' He shouted and opened his eyes. Thank God, he was dreaming. He pressed his hands on his temples and said 'No' again. He sat in the bed and shook his head violently. The movement woke Judith up. She saw the expression on David's face. 'Darling, it's all right. It's all right,' she said, hugging him and pressing his face to her chest. 'Thank God, it was just a nightmare,' he said.

'Was it the same one?'

'Yes, the same bloody one.'

David couldn't move his limbs. From the mounds in his garden, thousands of babies shot across the sky like a jet of gas, all on fire. The blazing jet ate the tender bodies. Their tongues stuck in their throats and terrible, choked shrieks were the only sound, an echo in that whitish dump. David's body started shaking again. God damn it. God damn it. He rubbed his eyes and said, 'Jud, the tablets.'

That nightmare started when he was four years old in Auschwitz. The tormenting memory was dug more deeply into his skin than the tattoo. Although he forgot about the number on his wrist, he would never escape the stench and the faces of the skeletal figure who were creeping between the huts. The ditches, the mud, the piles of excrement behind the blocks. David's skull exploded with pain. Judith handed him two pills and a glass of water.

'Try not to think about it,' she said. David tried hard to forget about what he had been through. He must not think about those agonizing memories. He looked at the patient Judith. Her breasts were emphasized by the dim light. The see-through night-gown clung to her slim body. David touched her shining hair with his fingers. Sighing, he pulled her warm body next to his and kissed the soft neck.

David drove to the town of Beer Sheva. Once, it was the Turks' administrative centre. David liked that city, although it was located in the middle of the desert. He got a lot of sun. Vitamin D. Good for the bones. When he was living in Zawichest, he wanted a lot of heat to make the cold of Europe evaporate from his body. His bones were getting drier and drier. One day, cracks would pave their way through his tanned skin. Through the sunglasses he looked at the sand dunes. It was blazing hot. Just bury an egg and it would be baked in a few minutes. A mirage? The Tiyahat roaming the Negev with their goat flocks and camel herds, the ships of the desert. That was what the Arabs called their dear camels. David pressed hard on the accelerator. Jud. He loved that slender woman, but he wished that she would stop being slim one day. What would happen if he went to the doctor? The same bloody tests, needles, pain and disappointment. 'I'm sorry, Mr Dzentis.' Sterile? Sterile?

He parked the car in front of Shalom Café. A cold breeze hit his damp face when he went in through the glass doors. He sat down, took off his sunglasses and dried his face and the back of his neck with his handkerchief. The hum of the air-conditioner mingled with the Hajjeh's velvety voice. David was developing a taste for Arabic songs, especially the Hajjeh, Um-Kulthom, although his Arabic was still not that good. The ebb and flow of the music coming from the loudspeaker fixed at the far end made him sway with delight. He tried to repeat with her that line. 'I tossed on the smouldering fire, and . . .' What? He couldn't understand the rest. And 'something, something' with ideas.

The dew drops on the red flowers smothering the cottages of Zawichest sparkled like jewels. What a pleasant smell! 'Turkish coffee, please,' he said to the waiter, who was an Arab. They were cheaper to hire, these bastards. The aroma of spiced coffee filled David's nostrils. Mmm. He sipped the brown liquid. David felt and saw better. In the glaring sun he could not see properly. Landscapes developed a hazy aura which caught the heat and reflected it. 'When they saw me, they said he had gone mad. I wish, I wish. . . ,' the Star of the East, Um-Kultom, chanted.

The picture of the crowd became clearer as if the focusing of David's eyes had been put right by the coffee and the cool breeze. Men and women chatted and laughed. Some repeated with the Hajjeh, 'I take the breeze for your step and the whisper for . . .' David remembered the ad he saw on television. 'The air-conditioning system transforms your summer into spring.' Nothing would transform Beer Sheva into green plains. Too salty, they said, and needs big quantities of fresh water. That was where the Canal of the Two Seas, the Dead Sea and the Mediterranean, came in. Agriculture would prosper when they build the Canal. David would plant his kitchen garden with flowers, the same red flowers of Zawichest, some mint, parsley and potatoes. 'When they saw me, they said he had gone mad . . .'

The slow rhythm of the song and the air-conditioner was shattered by a sudden explosion. The glass doors burst in, then smashed, showering the crowd with sharp pieces. David crawled slowly to a side window over bodies shivering on the floor. The shrieks of women would break all the window-panes in Beer Sheva. The bastards were attacking civilians again. Through the window, he saw three terrorists masked in black-and-white head-dresses, their khaki safaris loose around them as if to make them look broader. He searched the scene for rocket-propelled grenades. He found none. The RPG kids that time raided without their RPGs. Their legs were slightly open as they pointed their machine-guns at the café entrance, as if they were posing for CBS cameraman. Stupid kids. They started shooting again. All the women, children and men lay protectively on the floor under the clothed tables. The terrorists appeared fragmented through the café's broken window. They pointed at the end of the road, then retreated, shooting, to a car across the way. It picked up speed even before the terrorists had locked the side doors properly. Seconds later, two IDF jeeps arrived. The voices of the intermittent walkie-talkie and sighs of women filled the place, which was reduced to rubble. Husbands hugged wives and terrified children. Hysterical women were consoled by women soldiers. David's sunglasses had been smashed into small pieces. The bastards.

They thought that they would get away with it. They were dreaming. David pulled out his handkerchief and saw a cut in his finger. After all these years, his blood was still cheap. A public property that every shepherd used to graze his herd. They should be taught a good lesson. Was this the way to freedom or slavery? Of course, slavery to Marx and his teachings. They failed to see beyond their noses. They use Marxism as a veil to hide their thirst for blood. Stop philosophising and wrap up your finger. He tied his hand up, covering the cut.

They would never get away with it. The Shin Beit would dig them out like rabbits. They were one of the most efficient forces in the world, and if they did not find the terrorists they would shear through the silence of the Arab villages with their bulldozers. This would be better! The site would be confiscated by settlers. Then forts would be built. Laundry, skullcaps and children would fill the once-Arab village. The first bullet would be followed by a long series of actions. A bomb tied to a terrorist's waist would lead to a prisoner handcuffed to his jailer. A record was put on. Two IDF soldiers were beating up the Arab waiter with their rifle butts. The record began turning. David looked around him. Women, children, soldiers, the smell of ammunition, blood and coffee. A mess. What had that old man from Ma'alot said? 'There will never be peace in this ill-starred land.'

The Democratic State of Ishmael – Rahmah – 1977

One morning my mother woke up. She was exhausted. 'Working in that crowded place will kill me,' she said. Recently she had found a job in a biscuit factory. She had to put on a dark blue uniform and a white scarf and leave the house in the early morning. She told me that she stood in front of a big machine, collected filled biscuits and put them in a carton. 'Eman, today I am not going to work, I told the girls yesterday. Although I will lose a day's pay, I have to go down town and find a solution to the shop's problem. This is the third month that Sami hasn't brought us any money. Maybe I can squeeze some out of him this time.' She was out of breath when she finished talking. I decided to go with her.

'I'll come with you, mother.'

'Yes, yes. Bless you, child.'

We took the bus to Salaheddin Street. In the daylight, I looked at my mother's face. Yes, she was getting old. Something grabbed my heart and twisted it. A flock of birds were gliding across the sky. I wondered where they were going. I always wanted feathery wings to be able to soar high. To stand on the ground and start moving the wings, push and push until people and cars were reduced to ants. Were the birds lost? My mother touched me lightly on my shoulder. 'We are there,' she said. We walked on the crowded pavement. 'Delicious and cold. Liquorice root,' cried a peddler, clinking his glasses. Waving a blouse in the air, another peddler was singing loudly, 'For you, madam! Cheap, good and fashionable.' I dragged my mother to look at the window of a hardware shop. All the cups, plates, ash-trys, vases were sparkling like the brooch she had sold. 'Mother, is this a crystal cup?' I asked.

'Yes, love.'

I was looking for a cup like the one my aunt, Hanin, was accused of stealing from my uncle's house. The one in the window was like the prism the teacher showed us last week. Fascinating.

We went on walking for a few seconds on the pavement, then climbed a narrow staircase leading to a small shop on the second floor. Sami, Daddy's assistant, was sitting behind a counter talking to a young girl. When he saw us he stopped laughing. He walked quickly towards us and said, 'Welcome, welcome. Madam, you filled the shop with your light. And Miss Eman too. What an honour.' He pulled up two straw chairs and asked us to sit down. 'What would you like to drink? Pepsi? Tea?'

'Nothing, thank you,' my mother said calmly. I realized that my mother was tense. Oh, how we had changed after Daddy went to prison! My mother used to spend most of her time inside the house. 'Ladies do not walk around. Not too often at least,' Daddy used to say.

'Sami, since you haven't come to give me our money, I came to collect it instead. I said to myself, Maybe he forgot.'

'Madam, I am really sorry. I was very busy trying to pull things together. We are making a loss again. I don't know what to do. I spend most of my time here . . .'

My mother interrupted him. 'Do you mean to tell me that after my husband went to prison people stopped buying books? How interesting!'

'Things are changing. Our location does not help. Customers have to walk a long way to arrive here.'

'This shop was the best place for selling rare books. The income was enough for us to live a decent life. Now, look at us.'

'God help us, Madam. The tax people came back for more. I have to pay the book dealers, the Agency of Publication and, of course, exporters.'

'Sami, what are you trying to tell me?'

'I am afraid, Madam, I cannot give you more than ten per month.'

'You must be joking. What can I do with ten dinars?'

'I am sorry, Madam, but you have to understand my position.'

'Give me the money,' my mother said heatedly.

'Here you are. Thirty and an extra ten for sweet Eman.'

My mother snatched the money from his hand, took mine and went down the stairs quickly.

'What is wrong?'

'Sami is playing around and I cannot prove it. Oh, Mahmud, look what has happened to us during your absence. We've become a laughing-stock.'

On the way back from the shop, my mother was silent. I looked out of the window searching for the immigrating birds. I found none. On the right side of the street, a huge construction was built. It was a new automatic mill. Where were the green fields that used to be planted with vegetables? They used to be green all year long. I loved the wet smell of radish.

When we entered our house, my mother broke down and started sobbing. She put her hands on her covered head, then lowered it until it was placed between her knees. 'God, I cannot take any more. I just can't.' Her tear-drops trickled down to the bare floor. 'Your aunt is still an apprentice in that bloody beauty shop. Your uncle is just a soldier in the army. Also, he is saving to get married. What can I do? I can't even feed you now.'

I looked at my mother closely and said in a shaky voice, 'Mother.' My mouth was dry, which made it harder for me to continue. 'I don't want to go to school. Honestly, mother, they laugh at me there. They call me "the prisoner's daughter".'

My mother started crying loudly.

'Mother, I've thought about it. I even asked the teacher if there was a possibility for me to go back to school after some time. She said that I can sit for the high school certificate exam as a special student. So it is not the end of the world. Stop howling, for God's sake.'

'I wish I hadn't lived long enough to see this. I wish I was blind rather than see one of my children leave school. Oh, God of mercy.'

The tears were running down my mother's cheeks like a spring. I hugged her thin body and started patting her back gently. She was shaking like a scarecrow on a windy day. I knew then that she needed support and I was determined to give it to her. No school from that day on.

Um-Musaad found me a job as an apprentice to an Armenian tailor. I was to sew hems of dresses, serve coffee and tea and sweep the floor. It was not hard work. Sewing Lulu and for Lulu helped. The Armenian lady, Um-Arrtin, was pleased with my work. I started earning ten Ishmaelian dinars per month, plus some tips. The first time I handed my mother the ten dinars, she started crying again. I kissed her hand and said, 'Don't worry, mother. We will be all right.'

My work introduced me to the touch of silk and the odour of delightful perfumes. I used to see myself flying like birds wearing the colourful dresses I was sewing and ironing. Soaring high in blue silk, orange satin, printed georgette, crêpe de chine, chiffon, taffeta, velvet. Yes, velvet.

One morning, one of Um-Arrtin's best customers came. 'Hi, darling,' she said.

'Hello, dear. You look even more beautiful than the last time I saw you. What do you do to have such a smooth skin?'

'The Estée Lauder beauty expert came to Rahmah last week. I tried her. She was marvellous, but it cost me a fortune.'

'It must have been very expensive. Anyway, it is worth every piaster.'

She was still standing up, reluctant to sit down on one of the fading sofas. The yellow dress she was wearing had a black sheen. She took off her fur coat and gave it to Um-Arrtin, who took it very carefuly and put it on the sofa. The coat was a visitor too. The lady looked around, took off her leather gloves and sat down arrogantly. Whenever her necklace caught the light, hundreds of rainbows were released in the room.

'What would you like to drink?'

'Mmm, coffee, please,' she said in a clear voice.

'Eman, two coffees, please.'

I left the silk dress I was stitching and went to the kitchen. I overheard the woman saying to Um-Arrtin, 'Who is that disgusting girl?'

'Who? Eman. She is a neighbour of someone I know.

'She is so thin and shabby.'

'They're poor. God help them.'

My hands started shaking. I looked at my legs. I wasn't thin, or was I? I poured the Turkish coffee carefuly into the small cups, placed them on a tray and carried it to the sitting room. Um-Arrtin and the woman stopped laughing when I entered. I held out the tray to the lady, and the tray slipped out of my hands. Coffee stained the yellow dress.

'Look what you have done. Girl, don't you have eyes? Stupid idiot.'

I started crying. How dare she call me 'girl'? Um-Arrtin apologized to her customer on my behalf. Burning feelings grew inside me. I remembered Rida, Amal, Tal'at, Daddy . . . Oh, the burning flames. I was not 'girl'. I had a proper name. My name was Eman, Eman. How dare that woman call me 'girl'?

> 'Do you have sailors, captain,
> Dark and oriental, captain,
> Take us to our country, captain,
> To smell it's soil, captain.'

His father's voice grew thinner until it became the rattling of a dying man. 'Third regiment' was written in English on his khaki sleeve, emphasizing the British origin of his army uniform. 'The blond colluded with the crooked nose.' In the evening, while gathered around the campfire, they listened to his father's tales. Shadeed's lungs exploded. The black smoke in the cave blocked his view. Shit, he couldn't see Samir and Adnan. He was surrounded with flashes of dazzling light. Yes, the reckless sun was setting behind the mountains like a bellydancer. The red glow spread at the far end of the curved earth. His schoolmates gathered round the campfire, which had been lit in the widest alley between the tents. His father in his army uniform was singing between fits of crying. It was the fault of Abu-Huneik, Glubb Pasha, yes, his chin was broken. Shadeed's arm was broken too, you had only to finger his crooked elbow. Just one arm, one body, one person. Not enough. Futile, useless, void. The whip found Shadeed again and seized another morsel of his

91

oozing flesh. Betrayal of dignity, his brothers, his homeland, Palestine. The golden meadows were full of hidden lives which teemed under the brown soil. Indeed very fertile. 'Look at me closely, I don't care what the nurse in the Mother and Child unit said. She is American. Isn't she? I don't trust those UNRWA people. Even if it is going to kill you, I want more children. Do you understand? No, nine are not enough.'

Not enough had died, not enough had been born. Babies smeared with mud and their own excrement crawled in the alleys of the camp like worms. Adnan's sweet baby. Shadeed should see her and talk to her mother. He tried to get up. 'Uh.' A piercing pain hit him. What was the source of that pain? His rotten elbow? Stretch, stretch – no response. Shit. Where in hell was he? A very dark and gloomy spot. Another planet? Giant green insects carrying laser weapons rushed out of their bleeping space ship. Mechanical jaws moved, 'We-want-to-suck-your-juicy-brain.' Of course, Shadeed's mind was corrupted and stank like a rotten egg. Castro. Those who were not revolutionary fighters could not be called communists. For bread, for peace, for real freedom, for bread, for bread. White flour covered his mother's embroidered black dress. Layers of chalk dust on the sill of the blackboard. UNRWA warehouses and schools plus a blue card. The only connection with our house in Jaffa. Of course, they will return and the house would be handed to them exactly the way it was. The bubbling fountain in the yard reflected the blue sky. Twinkling stars decorated the sky of Nablus. Impossible, he was hallucinating. They had killed Samir and Adnan. Were they still alive? Hovering helicopters. Hungry eagles in the sky, searching for prey. A guerilla contingent that agrees to a truce in fighting is one condemned to defeat. Shit, no proper training. He wanted to move his body to shift the weight from the left side to the right, but quizzical blue eyes invaded his world. An iris started growing until the whole swollen thing was completely covered in blue jelly. The grotesque shape laughed: the noise infuriated him. Suffocate him, pierce the jelly with your scout's knife. Shadeed raised his right hand slightly, grasped the air, then his arm dropped to the floor. The sticky blue figure bounced closer: the space filled with reeking gelatine. Shadeed's neck jerked and he stammered, 'Go away . . . leave me alone . . . nothing, nothing . . . I know nothing.' His ribs tightened their grip on his lungs and quivering heart. Some air, some fresh air for the devil's sake.

Shadeed opened his sticky eyes and blinked to get a clearer picture. No use. All the solid shapes melted and escaped from him into the fog, increasing his isolation. He made out two containers in which some rice, a piece of bread and water had been thrown. He took a handful of rice and stuffed it into his mouth. The saliva ran from the corners of his distorted jaw. Another mouthful. Nourishing food poured down his throat. It was almonds and sugar to his tongue. Another mouthful. He felt content, full, dizzy. Eat the bread too. He chewed the bread with difficulty after swallowing the rice. The water tasted hot and salty like urine. Why not? Exhaustion overtook him and he leaned his back against the wall.

Where was he? He was in a dungeon with thick cement walls. The size of the cell was about one and a half metres by two. With his right hand, he touched the wall opposite him. Had it been scratched by human nails? The rugged surface reminded Shadeed of his mother's hand when he kissed it once in the festival. When would every living creature get bread, peace and freedom? He tightened his eye muscles to see the colour of the walls. Why were they brown. He moved closer and realized that the brownish layer contained shit and blood. Shit, man, shit. What was he doing there? He closed his eyes firmly in order not to see and cry. 'No eye see, no sad heart.' Reconnaissance mission. Near the top of the right side wall, an opening fitted with a zinc sheet allowed a faint light to creep through the slots.

What was out there? A merciless desert expanded, shrouding Shadeed with intense heat during the day and cutting cold during the night. He smelled the stink of processed minerals. Shit, the Zionists were robbing the wealth of the Dead Sea. Ashkenaz and Sephardim sunbathing in bustling kibbutzim. Once upon a time, there were hundreds of Arab villages out there. The aroma of chicken and spices covered with oil, onions and thyme filled the dungeon. They used to eat musakhen in the festival after slaughtering the two chickens they had. He wondered what his mother was doing. Perhaps running from one lawyer to another. Did the Nablus Military Governor order her to leave for the East Bank? Did she cross Damiya Bridge to be under the heel of the Arab countries instead of the heel of the Zionists?

The heels of the guard, who was singing in English, slid in circular movements. Shadeed saw the dancing heels through a narrow gap at the end of the firmly shut door. The guard was dancing and he had to sleep on this yellowish rubber mattress. Urine, that was it. He blinked at the filth on the floor. Night time? In the desert, it was easy to tell by the difference between the day and night temperature. Well, he would try.

Disgusted with himself, he spat on the floor. 'Shadeed, you make me sick, you coward. You're worried about your comfort and your brothers were burnt alive. You coward, you filthy rat.' He tried to stop his hands from shaking and spread the mattress from one corner to the other. In that way he got maximum length. He pressed his toes against the rough wall. When he tried to loosen his muscles, his body objected to the movement, so he curled himself again. 'You traitor, you led your brothers to their death. They wanted to leave the cave, but you didn't let them,' Shadeed reproached himself in a strong voice. His right hand was stained with Palestinian blood too. He rubbed it fiercely with the blanket. Traitor, betrayer, back-stabber.

Like a blind man trying to see his surroundings through the tips of his fingers, Shadeed touched his dishevelled hair. The curls stuck together, which made them easier to yank. On the top of his skull his hair was going thin. A big patch of rough skin was exposed. The widest alley in the camp. His lips were crushed and drawn back. Two teeth were missing. He put his tongue in the gap and licked the bare gum. One of his eye-sockets had swelled up with blood. Was that the reason for his blurred vision? At the back of his neck he could feel a cut like a net. David's filthy whip. He scratched his shoulders and realized that some parts were damp. Inflamed scars? Soap and hot water, priority number one.

He pressed his jaw. It had been hurting before. He ran his fingers through his thick beard. The bones were not broken. Under the feeble light he could see some blue patches on his belly. How many years had passed since he arrived here? His mother Hajjeh Amina used to say, 'It is much easier to knock down than construct.' Where was she? In Nablus or in one of the Arab countries? Even after her black braids grew grey, she rushed to UNRWA to get them some flour. Had she stopped praying to God that she buried his father in the right position? Hajjeh Amina, Um-Shadeed. The walls were like her hands, which made him feel closer to the cement.

The night before, his sleep had been disturbed by feathery touches around his mouth. He shook off the little creatures which were searching for food on his lips. Cockroaches or ants? Feelers were gliding gently over his skin. He shuddered and slapped his face. The pricks, imaginary or real, kept his only mobile hand occupied. Even when asleep, he scratched his shoulders and rubbed his nose in a frenzy.

He wanted to empty his bowels. He pulled himself up and squatted on top of the pail, waiting for the excrement to come out. His weak legs collapsed under his weight and he ended up sitting on the pail like a baby. Was he still Shadeed, who as far as he could remember was a mature, manly man? Never breast-fed. No diapers. Nothing. A bitter tear ran down his face, covering his bruised eye with salt. Shit, why was he crying? He didn't cry when they flogged him. He pulled up the remnants of his trousers and sat on the mattress. The smell penetrated through the opening. 'You did it,' said the guard sarcastically.

His left elbow was inflexible, so he tried to press his fingers to the palm, but the fingers remained stretched, indicating that his arm suffered from a fracture. The elbow was set in a V-shape, the forearm crooked near his chest. It should be straight and mobile. He knew what to do. No, he couldn't stand more pain. He just couldn't. The operation was a must. To push his forearm away from his body and to break the crooked shape. The sinking walls leaned on Shadeed. His eye-lids were wet with sweat. He had to do it. He grabbed his wrist with his right hand

and squeezed it until it turned white. He was a man, wasn't he? The sound of a soldier laughing, a cough, a dog barking in the distance. Gritting his teeth, he pushed his fore-arm violently, breaking the green bones again. His hand swung, unco-ordinated. When he was a young boy, he used to tie a stone to a rope and fling it towards the electric wires connecting the poles. The stone pulled the rope downwards. Soon, it would get entangled with the wires. As he drifted into a limbo, Shadeed heard the dog bark again in the distance. His 'Auliqa' missed the wires and flopped down to the ground.

The Democratic State of Ishmael – Rahmah – 1977

'Eman, I want to take you with me,' said my aunt one Friday morning.

'Yes, aunt.'

'"Hanin". Always call me "Hanin", not "aunt". You make me look ridiculous.' Her face started to collapse. The wrinkles around her eyes were cleverly covered with make-up. I used to spend hours watching her applying loads of coloured stuff to her face, and wondering where her original face had gone.

'A gentleman is going to pick us up and take us for a drive. Eman, I don't want you to tell anybody about it. Promise.'

The idea of a drive with a stranger made my imagination run. A tall figure would stop his car. I wouldn't be able to see his face. He would take us to a faraway place. 'Yes, a . . . Hanin, I promise,' I said excitedly.

'That's a good girl,' she said and put on her mulaya. 'I will go down town to do some shopping,' she said to my mother, who was cooking lentils with onions in the kitchen.

'Please, Hanin, you cannot go alone. What will people say about us? When the man went to prison, his women ran loose,' said my mother.

'Don't worry, I'll take Eman with me.'

'Good.'

'Eman, wash your face at least, for the devil's sake,' my aunt shouted at me.

She took my hand and we started walking. My feet were swollen when we reached a narrow alley, at the end of which a sparkling car was parked. The owner must surely have been working in one of the oil-producing countries. A visitor spending his vacation with his poor relative? My aunt said to me, 'Quickly – inside the car,' but my feet were stuck to the ground. She said, 'Come on,' and pushed me inside. She jumped into the front seat, the stranger started the engine, and we drove off. My heart was beating like the machines in the biscuit factory.

'I want to see your lovely face. Take off this silly mulaya,' the man said. My aunt pushed the black material off her head and looked at him. He took her hand and kissed it. I was shivering in the back seat as if a bucket of cold water had been poured over my head. I recognized the prosecutor who called Daddy 'a traitor' in the court last week. I shuddered and started weeping silently in the back seat. How dare my aunt talk to that man?

'I'll wait for you tonight. Don't be late, beautiful.'

'I won't. If you don't stick to our agreement . . .' she said, waving her finger threateningly. He held it, then kissed her finger gently.

'I want to go home,' I sobbed.

'Love, don't cry.'

'I want to go home, aunt.'

'We're going home. Don't worry.'

That night I couldn't go to sleep. Would my aunt slink out to meet that horrible man? She was lying in the only bed in the room. She kept tossing her head from one side to another. I could see my brothers' heads where they slept on the floor. My aunt started weeping suddenly, a strange suppressed sound. When our neighbour's cat was beaten, it cried in the same way. She got out of bed, wiped her tears, put on her black mulaya and tiptoed out of the room. Oh, God. She didn't know what she was doing. Suppose somebody saw her walking alone at that time of night. It would be a scandal to the Saqis.

I started counting the minutes in the darkness. When I heard footsteps outside I thought she had come back, but it was just a lost cat passing by. A dog was barking somewhere. Had it seen my aunt? My limbs were stiff like needles. The taut muscles of my back started hurting me. When would she come back?

The light of dawn entered stealthily through the window. Through my half-open eyes, I looked at the door. My aunt opened it carefully and slipped inside, then took off her mulaya. Her usually tidy hair was in a mess. Had she been running? She crept under the blanket and started weeping again. I rubbed my tired eyes and walked bare-foot to her bedside. I touched her shoulder and asked, 'What's wrong, aunt?' Her eyes were swollen and her lined face was not hidden behind make-up.

'Nothing, love, nothing,' she sobbed out.

'Please don't cry.'

She drew me nearer to her, hugged me and then squeezed me with her shaking arms. 'Oh, how I love you, Eman. Oh, how I love you and your brothers.'

The Democratic State of Israel – Beer Sheva – 1984

David found another terrorist waiting to be broken in the interrogation room. His name was Dirar and he was supposed to be a big shit from the headquarters. That son of a bitch infiltrated through the northern border coming for Khan El-Sheikh. Operation Peace for Galilee brought destruction and people like that bastard. From under the armpit of Russia they came to them, full-fledged birds. That Dirar was older than the previous one, Shadeed. The Russian bastards taught him all the tricks of the book after stuffing his head with vodka and rubbish, freedom, equality and bread, as if the Israelis had opened a national bakery to supply the Middle East. Why did the Jews always have to pay? David raised his hand and flogged Dirar, who was naked and handcuffed to two built-in loops in the wall. Dirar took a deep breath and started counting, 'One, revolution. Two, freedom. Three, strength. Four, victory. Five, the Return . . .' The bastard. David pulled his hair from the front of his scalp and said, 'In my life you do not occupy any space. You're a meaningless creature that lives on the margin of my days. So, hero, when I am here, be sure that I'll break your silence and get out whatever I want from you. Because when I am here in this room, breaking you is the centre of my life.'

David appreciated the improvements in the interrogation room. It made his job easier. He brought some salty water in a bucket and poured it into Dirar's mouth, compressing his jaws to prevent him from spitting or vomiting. The terrorist was well-built, but that did not mean anything. David's experience had taught him that external appearance had nothing to do with spirits. How many fat bodies had thin, thready souls? Dirar was swinging his body. The water tore his insides and peeled off the delicate tissues lining his stomach. Now was the time to use modern technology. David sprayed the terrorist's testicles and nipples with a strong chemical substance that caused burns of the second degree. Dirar vomited and his body jerked upwards, then downwards. He began whining like a thrashed dog rubbing itself on the doorstep of a kitchen. David pulled his hair again and said, 'What do you think? Do you like it? Do you want some more?' Dirar shook his head violently.

'Mo.'

'What?'

'No,' he stammered.

'Then, you will be a nice boy and give us a confession.'

Dirar shook his head again. David knocked his skull on the wall. Once, twice, until blood poured from Dirar's eyes. He nodded his head approvingly. Good. Good. The smell of vomit and blood made David's stomach turn upside-down. Although he was used to the stench of that room, the chemical stuff added a sharp, intolerable edge to the smell. 'Eh, a confession.' Dirar nodded again hysterically. 'Good. Sensible boy.' David unlocked the handcuffs, pulled a chair from the corner, and helped him to sit down. 'Steady, boy, steady.' He gave him a piece of cloth to wipe his face. In Dirar's coal-black eyes David saw naked fear. From a high and mighty commander, he was transformed into a dog struggling to survive. David shook some consciousness into him. The terrorist wiped the snot and blood from his face with trembling hands, gave David a military salute and smiled stupidly. Oh, how diferent was the commander from that young bastard, Shadeed! Young and silent. He detected some admiration in his memories of him, so he shook off the dust from his trousers to get rid of that feeling.

'Sir, he is ready,' David said to the senior investigator.

'Are you ready to give a full confession, commander?'

Dirar nodded approvingly. His stained chin touched the top of his chest. 'Soldier, bring him a cup of tea,' the officer ordered David. The terrorist could not hold the cup, so David helped him to drink the hot tea. He kept raising himself and sitting down. His arse must have been red-hot.

'Please, I want to cover myself up.'

'Of course.' David handed him a towel, and he wrapped it around his waist. His muscular arms were slashed cleanly and artistically. David was happy with the neat job. He was a master in his profession.

'OK, let us start from the beginning.'

Dirar cleared his throat and spoke in a shaky voice. 'The beginning was in Damascus. The network was organized there.'

'Who organized it?'

Dirar hesitated for one second, then whispered, 'Me.'

'Go on.'

'I sneaked through the northern border and came to Jerusalem where I recruited four young

103

men. I gave them money and some weapons that were smuggled in from outside.'

'Who smuggled the weapons?'

He stopped talking as if having second thoughts. David dug the wooden handle of the whip into his bruised side. 'Go on,' he shouted.

'Hajj Mansour from Beit She'an,' said Dirar calmly. He wiped his forehead while the officer was writing a note. He gave the message to the guard quickly. David could already see a bulldozer knocking down the houses of the peasants. The Settlers' Committee would zoom in, claiming the land, and Beit She'an would become a new settlement full of skullcaps. Why not?

Between stammering, pausing, speaking and fits of weeping, they managed to put together a coherent confession by the end of that day. To broken Dirar, the officer said, 'Let me read for you your confession. We must decorate it with your precious signature.' Dirar gazed at him with hollow eyes.

'In the night of 24th September, 1984, a terrorist cell fired Katyusha rockets at Jerusalem and failed to cause any damage. On the 25th, the IDF combed the Kasba of Hebron and the surrounding mountains and after a few minutes of sniping, arrested Ibrahim Musa, well-known as "Dirar", high commander in the P.L.O. Some terrorists resisted the arrest and were killed in the process.'

Dirar nodded violently and started weeping. His body flopped on the chair. Was he living an easy life? In a refugee camp? Impossible. The subdued sounds coming out of his split lips reminded David of something. What? What? From the depth of Dirar's heart, the sounds came helpless and desperate. Thus, the robust man was stretched to the very limits of his existence.

What a resistance movement! They teach them theories to apply, but as soon as they see their faces they forget Mao, Fanon, Giap and company. It would be better if the kids found another toy to play with instead of giving him a headache and themselves a heartache. Some of them did not know how to play with rockets and bombs and ended up blowing themselves into pieces. David stretched, satisfied with a day's work. He could see his promotion approaching. He was not that old, after all. He left the 'two commanders' chatting and went to drink his Turkish coffee. Sipping the brown liquid, he wondered what Judith had cooked for dinner. Baked potatoes and steak, he hoped. His forefinger was still bandaged. Probably next week, he would start working on the RPG kids who had raided the café and cut his finger. Always trust Shin Beit.

I asked the permission of Um-Arrtin to go to the court and attend the last session. My mother told me that the man who betrayed Daddy was going to testify. He was given another star for the information he gave to the authorities. Again using Habub's bus, we went to the court. I looked at the pillars. The spider was weaving its grey threads and tightening its net. When we entered the dark corridor the thin woman was still sitting on the wooden shelves. The old man was holding his stick firmly and the four children were gazing wide-eyed. We entered the hall, took our seats and waited impatiently. The judge read out a summary of the case and then summoned Captain Abdul-Qadder Lafi, senior officer in the Fourth Armoured Division of the armed forces.

A tall, lean man entered the court. He was wearing a sparkling army uniform. Three stars glittered on straps on each of his low shoulders. He went to the witness-box, took the Qur'an in his right hand and said, 'I swear by almighty God, to tell the truth, the whole truth and nothing but the truth.' His words rang confidently in the silent hall. The prosecutor began the questioning.

'Could you tell this honourable court the kind of information you gave to the Intelligence Department?'

Captain Lafi cleared his throat, twisted his thin moustache, looked around him quickly and said, 'I received an order to move my division to the capital. I suspected that there was something wrong. I contacted headquarters but couldn't trace that order. As a responsible citizen, I then notified the authorities in order for them to take the necessary action.'

Till then Daddy had been focusing his eyes on the same spot. I wished I could see what he was looking at. Suddenly he jumped to his feet and shouted, 'You liar! You traitor! May God's wrath be upon you!' A soldier pulled his arm and forced him back to his seat.

'Thank you, Captain Lafi. Indeed you have done your duty,' said the judge coldly.

Um-Musaad made sure that the lawyer would be in the court that morning. He rose to his feet and said in a weak voice, 'Your honour, may I ask the witness some questions?'

'Go ahead.'

'You said that you received an order. Who gave you that order?'

'I received it as a radio message.'

'And you instantly realized that it was a fishy order?'

'Yes, and checked with headquarters.'

'Your troops were actually moved from the base and found with their artillery four miles from the capital. Who gave them the command to move?'

The officer's face turned white. He looked pleadingly at the judge.

'The question is overruled,' said the judge, jotting down a note.

'But your honour . . .'

The judge looked at the lawyer threateningly and

said, 'Any other questions?'

'No, thank you,' spat the lawyer.

Daddy looked at the witness fiercely. Waving his finger, he said in a strong voice, 'Not just me, you atheist, but God, the oppressed, and the years will condemn you.'

The ticking of the electric typewriter stopped suddenly. The judge put on his glasses and asked, 'What's wrong now?'

'I don't know, your honour,' answered the shivering clerk.

'I told you, Risha, to do a typing course.'

'No funds, your honour.'

By then, all the people in the court had started laughing at poor Risha.

'I am not going to spend more time on this case,' the judge said impatiently. 'To hell with recording the proceedings.' He stopped talking, scratched his head and said, 'By the way. Who sold those complicated machines to us?'

'The company you recommended, sir.'

'Fine. Let's finish with this thing. I call upon the defendant to be cross-examined.'

The soldier made Daddy stand up. He faced the judge calmly. The prosecutor asked, 'How do you explain the paper we found in your house? Evidence number 3A, your honour.'

Daddy looked at the judge, but gave no answer. The lawyer started fumbling nervously with his papers.

'You are not going to answer. All right, the second question: Are you an active member of the National Freedom Party?'

'I was and still am. That is where your men have failed,' Daddy said in a strong voice still looking at the judge.

'So, you admit that you are a member of the banned party.'

'Yes . . . everything is written down in your report. Your men must have worked hard to supply you with all that paper.'

'Please, give precise answers. Have you or have you not visited on the night of 27 Ramadan the senior officer of the Fourth Armoured Division?' asked the prosecutor impatiently.

Daddy's hands were shaking slightly, a muscle in his cheeek was quivering. He stood firm and gave no answer.

'You are making this hard on both of us,' said the judge in his cutting tone.

'Hard on you, puppet. I bet the verdict is typed at the bottom of the report in front of you.'

The judge ignored Daddy's remarks, looked at the nervous lawyer, and said loudly, 'The counsel for the defence.'

The lawyer pulled himself together, picked up a piece of paper, and started reading. 'Your honour, the defendant standing in front of you is innocent. When young, he was tempted by a group of over-enthusiastic men to join the party. When he joined them he did not know that they would go this far. He regrets what he did and he is ready to sign a statement that denounces the Party's policy. I call upon your human feelings for his family. Giving him and his colleagues a capital sentence will stain the clean image of justice in this country. Mercy, your honour, and understanding . . . thank you.'

'The prosecution,' said the judge.

The man who had taken me and my aunt for a drive stood up and said, 'Your honour all the evidence shows that the defendant is guilty. He planned the coup, visited army camps and, on top of this, he

109

refused stubbornly to sign a statement!' He looked around him at the audience and continued, 'Your honour, ladies and gentlemen, this man penetrated through our armed forces, the Fourth Armoured Division, which was supposed to be moved to the capital at zero hour and start shelling the ruler's palace. One of our loyal officers told the Intelligence Department that a plot had been worked out, aimed against our dedicated government . . .'

Daddy interrupted him shouting, 'Traitors, mercenaries. The intelligence service of a western country discovered the so-called plot, not your loyal officers.'

'Shut him up,' ordered the judge.

A soldier struck him in the belly. He bent his body, winded.

I whispered through tears, 'I don't love him. Believe me, I don't love him.'

'He is going to use this honourable court as a platform for his decaying ideology.'

Abu-Ibrahim was suppressing his tears, my mother's were running down her cheeks, and my aunt, Hanin, was looking at her brother incredulously. She was utterly confused. The man started speaking again, 'Traitors like him should be given,' he cleared his throat, 'capital punishment. Yes, they should be hanged. All of them. Although we are a democratic state, your honour, high treason must be crushed with an iron fist.' My aunt opened her mouth stupidly. The three judges disappeared inside. Daddy was sitting on the wooden chair in the dock. Abu-Ibrahim raised his hands, looked at the ceiling and started invoking God. 'God, be kind to your loyal worshippers.'

'Amen, amen,' I said.

'God, they are weak and you are their supporter.

110

Help them and take their hands.'

'Amen, amen.'

My mother was speechless. Her dry eyes were fixed on the judges' door. Hanin was on the verge of fainting and Um-Musaad was threatening the lawyer under her breath.

'Stand up,' shouted a soldier.

We stood up, the judges entered and the verdict was read. 'The Martial Court convicts the defendant Mahmud Saqi of high treason against the ruler and the State and finds him guilty of the previously mentioned crime. Consequently, we order him to be hanged by the neck until he is dead on the 30th of this month in the mosque yard.'

'No, no,' I shouted, 'No, no. I hate him.' My mother fainted and fell on the floor. A triumphant smile spread across Daddy's face. Abu-Ibrahim started crying like a baby. Hanin became hysterical. Although her tears were pouring, she shrieked with laughter. Pointing her finger at the judges, she said, 'I gave everything I had to save my brother's life. Do you believe that? Everything, my gold, my treasures. Damn God. I wish God would fall to earth so that I could spit in his filthy face.' Yassin, the barber, ran towards her and dragged her out of the court.

Two soldiers dragged Shadeed through a damp, fetid corridor flanked on both sides with iron doors. Where were they taking him? Hadn't he had enough? His shaking knees collapsed, so one of the soldiers jolted his left hand. A piercing pain ran through his thin body. The pig hurt him, but he would not complain because the pig might yank his shoulder. He shut his mouth firmly and let his jailers pull him through the darkness. A door was opened and the soldiers pushed him inside. A dark room? Pain once again?

A smiling face said, 'Hello, Shadeed. How are you?' Shit, it was a new filthy trick. When the officer touched his left hand, Shadeed winced. His elbow. His elbow. 'Please Shadeed, sit down,' said the officer in perfect Arabic. Shadeed did not budge. The officer took his right hand gently and led him to a comfortable chair. How many years had passed since he sat on a proper chair? He loosened his muscles and filled his lungs with air. The wheel of time might stop and forget him sitting there. 'I brought you here because I have good news for you, my boy,' said the officer.

The strong light hurt Shadeed's eyes. All he was able to make out was a dark figure with no features. Shit, was he blind?

'A telegram from Rahmah arrived today through the Red Cross.'

Damn it. His mother had gone to Rahmah. Humiliation on top of humiliation. What was next?

'It's from Eman, your sweetheart.'

Eman? Yes, yes, Eman, of course.

'I'll read it to you.'

MY LOVE SHADEED I DO HOPE THAT YOU ARE ALL RIGHT STOP I WILL NOT LIE MY HEAD ON ANY OTHER ARM BUT YOURS STOP STILL WAITING FOR YOU STOP. Shadeed's heart started trembling in his chest. I MISS YOU AND YOUR PASSIONATE KISSES STOP. No way, Eman would never say that. He knew her well. She blushed when he kissed her for the first time. I AM COUNTING THE SECONDS TILL WE MEET AGAIN STOP THE SOONER THE BETTER MY LOVE STOP SHADEED BE SENSIBLE AND COME BACK TO ME STOP LOVE EMAN. Very clever indeed, however not original enough.

'Shadeed, look at me. The IDF captured Dirar, your hero, while combing the area of Hebron. He collaborated with his investigators and was given just a three-year sentence. What I want from you is just the names of the people who gave you the machine-guns. Easy and simple.'

Dirar? Impossible. No way. Shadeed forgot his blazing elbow when another kind of agony hit his heart. Impossible.

'Shadeed, this is your last chance.'

He couldn't believe that Dirar was co-operating with the Zionists. Impossible. It was another cheap trick. Was it? He couldn't distinguish between false and true any more. Exactly the same problem he faced during his exams.

113

'This is your last chance, mind,' said the officer, stressing every letter. The first or the last. Who cared? He always failed his exams anyway.

A big searchlight was switched on all of a sudden, blinding Shadeed. He should live up to his name and be tough. Earphones were put on his head. What was going on? What would they do to him? He prepared himself to join his brothers.

'For the last time, who gave you the machine-guns?'

For bread, for peace, for real freedom. Poetry:

> I am not a fortune-teller,
> I don't divine by views of sands,
> I don't read the stars.
> But I know that tyranny
> Is something passing
> And will never stay.

An electric current ran through Shadeed's body. 'No!' he shouted.

'Who was he?'

'No.'

Shadeed's surroundings began writhing violently. Every organ of his body was twisted and jerked out of its place.

'What?'

He stammered, 'Nnno.'

'Increase the voltage, soldier.'

A grating voice said, 'You are just a flea. We will put some electricity up your burning arse.'

The white flour diffused in the tent, covering every exposed surface. The balls were scattered then gathered, scatteredgatheredscattered.

The investigator looked so impatient. He kept hitting his palm with his fist, then scratching his head.

'Look at me, son of a bitch, I am very quick. They call me Magic Hand. My favourite entertainment is breaking souls. I am well-paid. You better work with me. It's fascinating to extract secrets even from dead men. I have everything at my disposal, dogs, electricity, chemicals, as well as psychologists. Shin Beit is one of the best in the whole world. Dig?'

Shadeed's perceptions were blunted. The words reached his ears as faint sounds and made no sense at all. The investigator wrenched his hair and said, 'I have many alternatives: to kill you, to make you crazy or to expel you. You have one simple choice: to confess.' The man's eyes were shining.

Shadeed lost his way in the vast desert. The blazing sun blinded him and the blowing wind deafened him. The dust rushed between the sand dunes like an evil spirit. The urge to dig a hole in the burning sands and to bury himself like the girls of Beni-Qureish took him over. They used to bury their daughters alive to tuck away 'shame' under the ground. Monotonous sounds coming from a distance pushed him towards his grave. 'Shadeed my son, your mother's heart,' his mother shouted. Her stretched limp hands welcomed him, connecting burning earth to hazy sky. Was it a mirage? Shadeed remembered other times and places when he sat on the cold floor between his mother and father. The bubbling fountain sprayed his dry face with water. The smell of citrus flowers and the twittering of sparrows seeped through him. His mother cracked with laughter at something his father whispered. He ran towards her saying, 'My mother, I am your son.'

'He started talking to himself instead of talking to us,' complained the investigator, slapping Shadeed's face. The vacant eyes looked at him. 'Look, tramp, forget about your Lenin and all this Russian stuff and come back to your senses. Because if you become disabled, your comrades will throw you in the street like a dog.'

'Democracy?' Shadeed murmured.

'You insist? You're asking for it!'

The investigator emptied a bottle into his anus. The liquid slashed its way down. Smouldering lava gushing from a crater. Then the pain eased, he was in the desert again, he was a tiny creature creeping across the sand dunes. The wind, the sun, the palm trees joined in a conspiracy against the crawling things. They did not bother to give him a glance. He went on digging the hole. His fingers bled profusely, so he licked the blood and continued his work stubbornly. Nothing would stop the tiny creeper from taking a short break. That was all he needed. He saw the limp hands stretched like a victory sign. 'Revolution until victory,' he said.

The earphones were put again on Shadeed's head. An electric shock went through him, tearing him apart.

'Talk,' the investigator barked.

'Dogs.'

'TALK.'

'Wandering bastards.'

'Talk.'

Shadeed's left hand became numb and he laid his body in the hole. Just some rest. His hand was covered completely with sand. His mother's arms urged him to get up. No, please, he didn't have the strength to stand up. The sand was warm and welcoming. The arms in the distance moved in a frenzy. He tried to get himself out of the hole, but his left arm did not respond. He raised himself, pulling his body upwards. He saw a black ant crawling on the yellow sands so he followed her, leaving his left arm shrouded in dust.

116

Shadeed trudged through the boiling sand. He looked at the horizon, searching for his mother's arms. He went on walking until the soles of his feet were peeling. Shielding his eyes, he looked at the black shape in the distance. The soot and smoke filled the space and blackened the yellow desert. His tears ran down his face and his lungs were torn into pieces. Blood gushed into bubbles, choking him and blocking the air outside his writhing body. While struggling for air, a group of disfigured children in white kaftans appeared from nowhere and formed a ring around him. Each was carrying a piece of his deformed body in his hand, freshly slain and dripping. An ear lobe, a wrenched thigh, an arm, jungles of bones, arteries, brownish blood, weals, slashed skin, and chops of meat. The trickling blood spread slowly over the white cover and then dripped to the ground. The faces had empty sockets. He was terrified, desperate to escape, but the dripping figures trapped him in a circle. They hopped and stood in a closed line like a chorus. They raised the dripping chops and made a collective gesture which meant 'You'. The blue lips jeered, then opened slightly, forming an O-shape. From the reeking mouths came a hissing sound, 'You, you.' Shadeed tried to run away, but they pulled him by his blouse and pointed at the smoke. 'You.' Shadeed raised his arms protectively to shield his face. Shadowy red figures were tearing him apart. 'No, not me, my father,' he screamed, 'my father.'

His father walked firmly towards him, still wearing his army uniform. 'Boy, I haven't sold our soil,' he roared. His usually smiling face and tearful eyes were decomposing. The bones of his skeleton were lined with a greyish skin. Bare joints and bones were reaching for him instead of the rough hands. The stink suffocated him and he cried for air, shutting out his father's figure. He tried to raise his legs, but they were stuck to the ground. 'Come on, move.' His feet came free and danced in the air, away from the reeking blood. His father's body and the dripping children were chasing him across the desert. He was on the very edge of an abyss. The eyeless faces hissed, 'Fall down, go down.'

'Please, help me,' Shadeed begged his father.

His father walked calmly towards him, then, with his skeletal hands, pushed him. He lost his balance and fell into the dark opening. The noise of his father's laughter echoed in the abyss. Blue shrieks, hollow, fading . . .

'Shadeed, my baby, don't take off your shoes tonight.' He did not know what his mother meant but he cried. He saw his mother pushing his brothers out of the tent. He slipped under the blanket and covered his head, shutting his eyes firmly in order to forget about the darkness around him. Bang. A shocking sound woke him up. He called, 'Mummy, Mummy.' No answer. 'I want Mummy,' he cried. Enveloped with the blackness of the night, he wept and screamed, 'Mummy, Mummy.' A flash of fire lit the place, then exploded, taking half of the tent with it. Shadeed's tender body shook with fear. He stood up and walked around the rubble calling his mother, 'Mummy, where are you?' He began weeping again. His shrieks filled the camp but still nobody took any notice of him. He went on and on for hours then fell down to the ground exhausted. Near the dying fire that ate up half of his home, he sat sucking his thumb.

His mother came pulling his father's body. He ran to her and tried to grasp the end of her dress, but she pushed him violently. He started crying loudly. She yelled at him, 'Shut up.' He stopped crying. Another woman helped his mother in placing his father under what was left of the tent. 'It is another catastrophe, my sister. They will force us to leave again. So, my sister, I want to bury the father of my children properly,' said his mother and started sobbing silently.

'Hajjeh Amina, I will help you.'

Shadeed's mother brought a bucket of water. She stripped his father and poured water over his body, then scrubbed. 'Could you believe it, the wound in his chest is still bleeding.'

'A martyr. Paradise will be his haven.'

His mother took off her white veil, tore it into two and tied it around the bleeding body. 'Now, what should we do? I think we should lie his head towards Mecca.'

'How could we tell the east from the south in this mess, my sister? God is forgiving. Just place his head wherever you can.'

'Let us dig a grave first. I have hidden his axe somewhere. He used it for digging waterways in our plantation in Jaffa.'

His mother brought a rusty axe and started digging vigorously.

'My turn,' said the woman, taking the axe from his mother.

A hole was carved out and they both carried the limp body and placed the head towards the road leading to Jerusalem. 'That is the only reasonable thing to do.' His mother recited some verses of the Qur'an, then pushed the soil over his body. 'I pray to God that I have buried him in the right position.' She looked at the dying fire and said, 'God make the Jews' houses collapse over their heads. Amen.' She

119

took Shadeed's hand and ran with the other women to the UNRWA school. 'At least he is buried in Palestine as he always wanted.'

'Yes, Hajjeh Amina.'

His mother released his hand and started slapping her cheeks. 'Where is the school, my love? Where is the school, my heart? It was here, my sister.' She cried hysterically and repeated the same question over and over again. Shadeed joined in. 'My God, I wish I was with you, my beloved. My mother, my heart, my heart. Your father and then you, my children.' She looked at the woman and asked, 'What do I do, my sister?' She pulled off what was left of her white veil and started waving and jumping as if dancing. 'My God, my beloved, I wish I went with you. My children, why did you go and leave me here alone? Why?' She yanked her hair and uttered long-drawn, thrilling sounds as if it was a wedding not a funeral. 'Ya Ya Ya Ya.'

The Democratic State of Ishmael – Rahmah – 1977

Aunt Hanin spent hours and hours howling frantically. When she recovered, a wild look stayed in her eyes. My mother collapsed and spent four days in bed. She suffered from a fever and was hallucinating most of the time. When I placed a wet piece of cloth over her forehead, she smiled at me and said, 'Amal, my love, you're back.'

'We must do something. We cannot sit around and let them hang him,' my mother said to my aunt and Um-Musaad one week later.

'I did my best,' said Hanin.

'Look, we tried demonstrations and appeals. Activities inside are not paying off. Yes, why not send telegrams to all the rulers of the Arab countries,' said Um-Musaad.

'Vinegar is the brother of mustard,' said Hanin.

'Yes, I know. But at least we could try.'

'Eman, bring a sheet of paper and a pen – quickly,' said my mother.

I sat down ready for dictation. 'Write down,' said Um-Musaad,

'Your Majesty/Mr. President:
On behalf of sixteen families in the Democratic State of Ishmael, we send you this appeal. We beg

you to intervene and stop the massacre that will take place at the end of this month. Sixteen innocent men will be hanged and at least eighty-six children will lose their fathers. In the name of Allah, the Beneficent, the Merciful, He who has done an atom's weight of good shall see it. And he who has done an atom's weight of evil shall see it.'

'Um-Musaad, you are digressing. You know how much that will cost us?' Hanin said heatedly.

'We're broke,' said my mother.

'Why not collect some money from the neighbours?' I suggested.

'Do you think they will sympathize with us?' asked my mother.

'I know how to make them pay,' said Um-Musaad clenching her fist.

'He did what he did for them,' said my mother.

'But who understands that? Nobody, nobody,' said Hanin.

Shamma'eh was a thin, short garbage collector. His body was V-shaped as if struck permanently on the stomach. Other people's trousers tied around his narrow waist looked like an inflated parachute. He did not believe in growing hair so his bald, shining skull inspired a respectable neighbour to nickname him Shamma'eh. 'A candle that will always give us light,' he said. Shamma'eh was a heavy smoker, not very heavy though because his cigarettes were merely butts picked up from the sweepings.

When I saw Shamma'eh that morning, I asked him for a donation. I explained to him that we were sending telegrams to Arab leaders asking them for help.

'Don't get too close to the cat. You might be scratched. Rip off the cat's head in the wedding night. It is absolutely like that, which means that it's no use at all, and the whole thing is useless. Isn't it?'

'Yes, Shamma'eh, whatever you say.'

'It's futile. Among this rabble and filth, where do I stand? In the garbage, of course. I will pour all those black sacks over my head and rub my skin with filth. The more garbage in the city, the cleaner it will be. No imperialistic democracy. No, nothing. Yes, I will pay dear, sweet Eman. Stick to the garbage. Here you are.' He slipped his hand behind his belt and took out a wrapped bundle.

'Twenty dinars? Are you crazy?'

'I am. I wanted to get married. I have been saving for three years. No problem. I'll start again.'

'Shamma'eh, are you sure?'

'I am sure I am garbage, filth, dirt, and down with imperialistic democracy. Play something and I'll dance.'

He started drumming on the door with his slim fingers and singing,

'A grain up there,
A grain down here.
Hey, people of up there,
Sympathize with people down here.'

I took the money and left Shamma'eh dancing to his strange tunes in the morning light: a marionette shaken violently by an impatient puppet-master.

When he heard Shadeed's cry, David was leaving the prison building. Was it Shadeed's voice or his imagination? He cocked his head, listening. Nothing. He turned round and went down the steps leading to X-Section. He took off his sunglasses because the corridor was dark. They must be busy, judging by the moans and cries of prisoners. 'I would like to see Shadeed, soldier.'

'Why do you want to see this son of a bitch? You finished with him, didn't you?'

David shrugged his shoulders and the guard, impressed with his nonchalant manner, opened the cell door. The pail was empty and the food container was untouched. 'When did you empty his pail?'

'Three days ago.'

David looked at the prisoner. Why was he lying naked in his excrement? His body was curled like a worm on the stinking mattress. His pale face was covered with flies which fluttered their wings and licked the leftovers around his lips.

His left arm was limp. What was wrong with it? David knew that he had caused some injuries but not that serious. He pulled Shadeed's fingers, then dropped his hand. The arm drooped like a piece of cloth. Puss and blood oozed from the wounds on his back. The deep red skin showed that the cuts were inflamed.

They had shaved his head and beard. With his right hand, Shadeed rubbed his nose in a frenzy, then began moaning, a submissive sound with a sad edge. There was something odd about his whimpers. Something out of this world. David shuddered. It seemed to him that the boy was in danger. How could he convince the authorities? A medical check-up was urgent, as far as he could see. He touched the man's forehead. Hot – definitely fevered. His black toenails worried David. Was he responsible for these black spots? A scar ran on Shadeed's bottom like a trail of smoke. Well, they had used that hellish substance. As a last resort. The guy had given them a hard time. His shaking body jerked the mattress with each movement. 'You keep bringing him fresh food without bothering if he eats it or not?'

'Who cares about him, man?'

'He has a fever, he's unconscious.'

'So what?'

'He needs medical treatment urgently.'

'That's not my fucking business.'

'You should report whatever goes on inside this bloody cell.'

'He is unconscious most of the time and some of the time crying. There is nothing to report.'

Shadeed didn't cry even in his darkest moments. 'You must report his condition.'

'He was thrown here to bring some sense into his head. As long as he resists, he should, as far as I am concerned, rot in this shit-hole.'

David looked at the deformed, shaking skeleton which he had helped to create.

'Thank you,' he said, and went out quickly. He put his sunglasses on. The sandy yard of the prison reflected the heat and intensified it. David wished he hadn't gone back to see Shadeed. What was the use?

125

In five months, at least ten years had been added to Shadeed's age. David wished that all the Palestinians could disappear from Israel at a single stroke of magic, without his forcing them towards their graves.

David kept thinking about that shaking skeleton. The image of Shadeed's bald skull and the fly-covered lips haunted him day and night. Finally he made up his mind. The next morning he would go to the prison's doctor and discuss the matter with him. Possibly, he could do something to save the poor bastard. What would they say about him giving a hand to an Arab? Not just any Arab, but a terrorist too. He did not care. He would go all the same. Driving people up the wall was his job, but not burying them in the bloody wall.

The next morning, he entered the clinic and realized that it was the cleanest spot in the whole stinking building. It got some sun, which made it warm. Seconds later, Dr. Unna entered the room. He was bespectacled and untouchable in his white robe. 'Yes, David, what can I do for you?' he said in a cold tone. David hesitated. 'Do you want me to prescribe more tablets for you?'

'No.' David shook his head. He pulled himself together and said in a shaky voice, 'I came here to ask about one of the prisoners.'

'Really? Who?'

'Shadeed.'

The doctor scratched his head and said, 'Yes, the boy who went mad last week. Mmm, what about him?'

David was infuriated by the doctor's attitude: he was acting as if one of his rabbits in the lab had died. 'When you discovered that he had broken down, what did you do for him?'

'Who are you to question me like that?'

David controlled his anger and said, 'I am just asking.'

126

'I gave him an injection of insulin.'

'When?'

'The second day.'

'So, the guard did not report his collapse earlier?'

'Yes.'

'Why didn't you go that night?'

'Look, David, he's here to break down.'

'He's here to collapse and give some useful inform-ation, not go mad'.

'I did what I could.'

'What will happen to him now?'

'I will examine him thoroughly and write a report on his condition. Further action will be taken in the light of it.'

'Do you think he'll ever get better?'

'Honestly, no.'

'So, what will you recommend for him?'

'Some sedatives and transfer from X-Section.'

'He's finished then.'

'Taking all the symptoms into consideration, I would say, yes.'

'Thank you, doctor.' David could not understand.

'Say hello to Judith.'

'Yes, I will.'

David was completely mixed up. Incidents had lost any logical colour called meaning. So, the poor kid had gone mad. David cracked into laughter. 'The worst calamity is what brings laughter,' the Arabs say. Shadeed wanted to be a hero, immortal. Look what happened. Better forget about him, he was beyond help. How he wished . . . No, God damn it. He walked across the yard, then turned and looked at the old building. The white and blue Israeli flag was fluttering. No matter what, he would protect his country at any cost. He would readily give his life to keep that flag on top of that old building. Yes, he would give his life.

At the end of his shift, David went to see Shadeed. He ran down the steps of X-Section. The kid had been fine a few weeks ago. It seemed to David like years. 'Hello, soldier.'

'Hello, sir.'

'Were you here the night Shadeed was ill?'

'Yes, sir.'

'What exactly happened?'

'I was standing in front of the prisoner's cell as usual, listening to the radio. There were these strange noises. I switched the thing off and listened. The prisoner stammered out something or other. I thought he was dreaming, but the noises grew louder. So I opened the door. And the guy was writhing like he was split into two. His head was shining with sweat. He could not speak, his neck was jerking too much. And he had this fixed stare, and dull eyes. He pushed, like he was fighting something strong. I have never seen anything like it in my whole life, sir. Well, while I was looking, he stopped trembling, and lay down on the floor and went to sleep.'

'Did you report it right away?'

'Yes, sir, but nobody came that night. God help me, the next morning, I opened the door to fill the container. The prisoner was relieving himself on the mattress. He gave me an empty look and spoke to me like a child.'

So, David thought, he hadn't taken a few years off Shadeed's life; he had wiped them nearly all away. 'What did he say?'

'"I don't want to play with you, I don't want this food." Things like that.'

David looked inside the cell. Shadeed was playing with an invisible toy. 'Shadeed,' David whispered as if talking to a rabbi in a synagogue. Shadeed tried to detect the sound and slowly turned his bald head. A glimpse of fear – then a mask dropped over his eyes.

'Go away,' he said in a hissing voice.

'Shadeed, don't you recognize me?'

'No,' Shadeed said. Then his pupils dilated and he said, 'Mmm. Yes, you are my father.'

David could not speak.

'I wished that you would come sooner,' said Shadeed reproachfuly. 'You, my father, my real father, I commanded you to come.'

The cell was nauseating. The dampness and the shit made breathing impossible in the narrow space.

'Why didn't you come before? You could have prevented them from pushing me. He was with them, but he's not my real father. You are.'

David kicked the iron door with his black boot, then pushed his blond hair away from his forehead and said as calmly as possible, 'Yes, my dear boy, I am your father, and it's very true: I should have come earlier.'

David climbed the steps of X-Section, slurring his boots on the filthy floor. Slowly, he took out his sunglasses and tried to fix them into place. The rim hit the peak of his cap, so he threw the glasses as far away as possible. What in hell had he done? Anger boiled inside him, trying to bubble out. The Khamasin wind that blows in the desert and changes the shape of sand dunes would be coming in seconds. A sharp headache exploded in his skull. The waves took a new pattern. He sat down on the sand near the main gate of the prison. Shielding his eyes, he focused on the very far end of the golden tableau expanding in front of him. 'What is your name? David Dzentis. How old are you? About 39.

Where did you come from? From Zawichest in Poland. How long have you been here? Twenty-seven years. What in hell are you doing here?'

Here he was after all these years, sitting on the ground, talking to himself, hunting for the dusty mirages in his head. His life spread like scattered palm trees or like a pool in an oasis. The trees were lost in the barren scene, they were hardly noticeable. Merely some small green dots in the golden ocean. They would sink.

Suffocated by the heat, David opened the first three buttons of his khaki shirt. The thought that he would never have a clan of his own made his heart as heavy as a rock. Few shoots to add greenery to the scene and fight the dryness of the desert. The sand waves would engulf the buildings some day. Damn it, if he had children, he would have quit his job and gone with them southwards to the desert to start a settlement. The Khamasin would arrive soon and transform the shape of the sand dunes. David looked at his forearms and noticed that his tan was getting darker. The cut in his forefinger had healed at last, leaving a white thread. How many such reminders were carved on his skin?

His lids were getting heavier and heavier. Sleep is a sultan. He leaned his back against the prison wall and tried hard to keep his burning eyes open. He drowsed off and saw the jet in his garden. The children shrieked and cried. The trail of smoke became darker with human remnants. He woke up suddenly and found himself face to face with the sands. The sun was sinking in the dust. Would it give light and life to other worlds and people? It seemed to him that he had lost his way and finished up here, asleep. He shook the drowsiness out of his head and struggled to place himself in the complex jigsaw.

Where was the fading green dot in all that golden tableau of waterless desert?

'They'll hang him today,' said my uncle calmly. 'Sister, neither you nor your children are allowed to leave the house. Do you understand?'

'I want to see him for the last time. Please,' said my mother.

Uncle placed his fingers under my mother's chin and looked at her in the eye. 'It's for your own good.'

I could not believe what my uncle said. After all the blood and tears we had shed, they were going to hang Daddy. I simply could not believe it. If I didn't see it happening with my own eyes, I would live all my life convinced that he was still in prison. I wanted to say good-bye to him. No. No. God would not allow it. At the last moment, an answer to one of our telegrams would arrive and stop the execution. Yes, I was sure. But I had to be there. The mosque yard, they said. I would go no matter what. That raging uncle did not frighten me, though he frightened my mother.

I sneaked out of the house and started running down the hill. If I went on running in that direction, I would end up in the valley, down town. I was out of breath. My eyes were burning from the cold wind. Go on! I caught a glimpse of my surroundings and realized that the whole town was moving downwards. So, they would turn out to watch the scene. That morning, only three of the condemned sixteen would be hanged. No. No. It was not possible. I was sure the whole thing would be cancelled. God of mercy, give them ease and help them in their ordeal.

The yard was crowded with people. I squeezed through until I reached the first line. 'Careful of pickpockets,' I heard a man saying. Sheiha, the baker's roundsman, was there with his sesame cakes. 'Coffee, coffee. Hot and refreshing,' Zarour, the coffee cook, was shouting.

In the middle of the yard, right in front of the ornamental mosque gate, a wooden framework had been built. At the right end of this table-like structure a wooden ladder was fixed. Some ropes were swinging in the cold wind. A skinny man with a masked face climbed the steps lightly, fitted the ends of ropes to hooks and descended. A black vehicle stopped near the mosque. It had no windows at all. A soldier opened a door in the back and pushed out three ghostly figures. They were completely covered in white. I recognised Daddy because he was limping. All three were handcuffed. The hangman patted their shoulders one by one, urging them up the steps. Daddy was the first to go up. Slowly, Daddy, slowly. The whole thing would be cancelled, I was sure. God would forbid it. When he reached the top, he raised his right arm and said, 'May peace be with you.' The second man followed Daddy steadily, but the third collapsed and had to be carried up.

Daddy was reciting verses from the Qur'an in a loud, clear voice while the hangman was fixing the rope around his neck.

'In the name of Allah, the Beneficent, the Merciful . . . Surely the guilty are in error and distress. On the day when they shall be dragged upon their faces into the fire; taste the touch of hell. Surely We have

133

created everything according to a measure. And Our command is but one, as the twinkling of an eye. And certainly . . .' The hangman raised a lever and crash went the table. The three bodies fell, came up with a sudden jerk and then began swinging limply in the morning breeze.

I lost my balance and fell to the ground. 'Mummy, Mummy,' I cried. The crowd was motionless as if struck collectively on the skull with a huge hammer. I saw Abu-Ibrahim in the distance. His hands were stretched towards the grey sky. I rose to my feet, ran towards him, grasped the front of his army shirt, and shouted, 'You son of a bitch! You bloody bastard! After all this you're still invoking God. He's deaf. Do you hear me? Deaf. Deaf.'

I was shuddering like a slaughtered chicken. I couldn't see or hear anything. It had not been cancelled. A big lie. A joke. Oh, how could they? I fled the stench of the yard and started running around in circles. I stood on the pavement gasping for air. 'Victory Public Bath' was written on an iron gate. I pushed it open and entered.

'Hey, where do you think you're going?' a man wrapped in a towel said. 'This place is for men only.'

'I want to have a bath,' I said.

He examined my shabby appearance and stained face and said, 'OK, you are not a woman anyway. Use that cubicle, and keep the curtain well-closed.'

I pushed the curtain open and went inside. The bath was spacious, and full of steaming water. I took off my clothes and stepped in. Two legs gazed back at me, spread in a V. Were they broken? I plunged my thin body into the hot water and started massaging my muscles. Brown dirt trickled down my limbs and stained the water. The cubicle was shrouded in steam. I felt I was washing my tired body inside a cloud. My eyes misted with tears, scalding tears that started running on my cheeks, burning their way down. Flames blazed up inside . . . Rida, Amal, Tal'at and Daddy. He lied to me when he said that Daddy would come back. Now, he could not come back. I immersed my head in the water too. A small fish in an endless ocean, completely enveloped in murky water.

'1,2,3,7. No. No, stupid ass. 1,2,3,4.' Right. 'Now, try counting to ten. 1,2,3,4,5, . . .' Shadeed wanted to impress the ladies in the big house. He sneaked there while they were drinking their morning coffee. Once, he pinched the rounded leg of one of them, tempted by its fullness. 'Heh, heh.' 'A: Anti-imperialism, B: Better future, C: Come with me, D: Deeds speak louder than words, E: Eden for martyrs, F: Failure to my enemies, G: Gentle with my friends, H: Tra-la-la.'

The guard opened the heavy door and replaced the containers. Shadeed pushed away the food container and pouted. His eyes were vacant and his expression was fixed. In a child's voice he said, 'I hate this stuff.' The guard shuddered. 'Why do you look at me like that? Go away! Go away!' The guard rushed out of the cell and closed the door. 'Heh, heh.' Shadeed looked for something to amuse himself. He found a black ant striving to cross the room. He picked her up and placed her on his palm. 'Why did you come here? You want to sting me. I know that. Leave me alone.' He placed her on the ground and pushed her forward. 'The ant said to the cicada who was chirping shrilly all the summer, "While you were singing, I was collecting grains, lazybones. Since you have sung during the summer, you can dance now." Our master, our master, God protect our master.'

'Where are you, smart-ass?' He searched for the ant again. He had asked his father, his real father, to come, but he never did. 'I, God almighty, command you to come. Don't pretend that you're not listening. I can touch you.' He felt that the ant wanted to drag him out and bury him in her teeming nest. 'Shadeed, Shadeed, Shadeed. Me, I am Shadeed.' She'll step on him, but the cave was empty. He wished. He wanted to kill himself. What was the use of living? Slash his neck with his scout's knife, but he did not have a neck. 'Heh, heh, stupid.' Shadeed stretched his right hand and waved to the ant. 'Come, come, my darling, I've kept some food for you. Eat, eat quickly before they see us.' He laughed hysterically and said, 'That's a good girl.'

His school books flew in the air like pigeons. He loved stealing oranges from the big house. 'Palestine is our country and the Jews are our dogs.' His mother was waving her white veil and uttering shrill sounds. What happened to his father? 'He is a martyr and God will protect him. God will meet him in heaven.' What had happened to his brothers? 'They are the sparrows of Paradise. God will meet them too.' Shit, God was dead. 'A,B,C, 1,2,3.' The cave was closing in. It was cold and damp. The air was still. He couldn't breathe. He was sitting on the mud and stones with his brothers. A huge rock closed the cave-mouth. He was imprisoned in that shit-hole. The stink filled his nostrils. Fresh air. He couldn't run away or breath. The smoke from the fire suffocated him. He pressed his chest with his hands. To cut his neck open, that was it. A fluid. Rushing water pushed the rock and flooded into the cave. Shadeed would sink soon. No breathing. No escape. The level of water rose rapidly. He would drown in the rising fluid. Wait. He looked around. Shadeed was not in the cave. It was empty. No, not completely empty. A black ant was hissing near the damp wall.

The ant crawled back to Shadeed's cell. 'Coming for more food, my darling?' he asked her kindly. He gave her his right hand, then picked her up with his thumb and forefinger gently, making sure not to press hard on her tiny body. Studying her closely, he discovered that she was not black, as he had thought, but dark brown. Shit, the light. She had two feelers and brown, swollen eyes. 'You got jaws too,' he said, surprised at the rapid movement of the grinding pieces. 'You are lucky because you have a lot of joints.' Hair covered the ends of her six legs. She raised herself up on her hind feet, bringing her abdomen between her legs. 'What is wrong with you? Do you want food?' Shadeed listened carefully to the moving mouth and heard a hissing sound. 'Yes, yes, of course.' He put her back and from underneath the rubber mattress he took out a handful of rice and put it in front of her. 'I kept those for you, my darling.' Pulling a grain of rice, she proceeded on all six legs towards an invisible hole in the cell wall. 'Very wise, my darling. Please come back.'

Curled on the floor, he saw her creeping towards the rice again. 'Hello! How is the weather outside?' He listened to her hissing. 'Is it cold then and windy, poor soul? Do you live far from here? Just a few yards from my place. Good, good. What did you say? You are inviting me to your home. Of course, my darling, one day I will come.' Shadeed crawled over to empty his bowels. The excrement cut its way down, opening all the old scars and splitting him in two. Shit, that pain again. Suppressed tears trickled down his throat, leaving a lump behind them.

He sat down in the excrement and tried hard to focus on the cave. They wanted to kill him but he

vanished completely. Shadeed, Shadeed, him, he
was Shadeed. 'Ya Ya Ya Ya. Go away, I hate you.'
He wished that the water would engulf him, but he
disappeared, evaporated.

'Do you have sailors, captain,
Dark and limping, captain?
The sea is shit, captain.'

Him, he really was Shadeed. She came and went
and came and went. She made him sick. How could
you be sick?

Someone opened the door and brought in food.
He started and said in a hissing voice, 'Who are you?'

'A friend.'

'Knock on the door before coming in.'

'OK, whatever you say, man.'

'Why are you gazing at me like that? I am God
almighty. You never saw him before.'

'No, man.'

'Out, out, shitty dog.'

The man went out and closed the door of the
room, leaving Shadeed with his darling. He asked
her to stay, but she insisted on going away to sit her
exam. He wished that she would come back and hug
him. He shrieked with mad laughter because he had
managed to cheat them all. They thought they were
cleverer than him. Look what happened! Nobody
could harm him, they simply could not. He was
invincible. 'I am your God and you must obey my
orders.' A white patch had stuck inside his eye, it had
been there for days. He rubbed his eyes, but still the
picture remained as blurred as the camp television.
He longed to see her when she came back so he lay
flat on the mattress, waiting. 'Here you are. You
took longer than usual. Why, my darling? I've been

thinking about your invitation and I've decided to visit you. Yes, soon. Do you have grains for everybody? Then, sure, I will come.' She answered in her hissing voice, 'You are welcome,' moving her feelers gently over the grains of rice.

Shadeed shuffled his feet on the sands under the heat of the orange circle. The dunes extended in front of him like the waves of a vast sea. A wind hit his face, carrying burning grains of sand. The dryness of the place suffocated him and made him loll his tongue far out like a thirsty dog. The sun's heat blazed and made his skull wet. He saw his mother's arms stretched out. A mirage? Children in their white kaftans pointed their distorted limbs at him. He saw a cloud of smoke in the distance. The ghostly figures of his brothers, Adnan and Samir, emerged through the blackness. Their eyes were hollow, without any warmth. He ran towards them to hug them. They refused to shake his hand. He dropped his head and asked, 'Why?' Samir and Adnan shook their heads and said nothing. 'Please, tell me why,' he pleaded. 'You know how much I love you.' The two figures roared with laughter. Shadeed began weeping bitterly. The tears evaporated as soon as they touched his lashes. What was wrong with them? They didn't frighten him at all. The wind grew stronger, brought up clouds of sand, then dropped them down in fresh shapes, ridges, breasts, skulls. A dusty hell advanced towards Shadeed. Dust shrouded the faces of Adnan and Samir, so Shadeed got rid of their accusing eyes. Hit by a blast, he lost his balance, fell down, and wetted the dry soil with his tears. The heat that melted the sands enveloped him. He shut his eyes tight to protect them from the flying ash. It scalded his back. He would be baked alive. More ashes, more burns, more flames. Fight, push, pull. A huge force pushed him down. Deeper. Deeper. Stinging grains stormed into his ears, eyes, nose, mouth until he inhaled burning sand.

Like the break of the first sunbeam after a long night, his body became amazingly lighter. The pressure and the piercing wind eased. He woke up and looked around. The rubber mattress, the pail, the food container, the blankets were still there. He searched the room for Shadeed, but he was not there. Where had he gone? The room seemed empty. He focused his bulging eyes on his legs. Yes, two extra legs were coming out from each side of his body. So, he had six legs, each with two joints. Marvellous. He inserted his head into the food container and sucked some rice. His jaws ground down the food swiftly and his bald skull joggled. He gazed at her and said in his hissing voice, 'Hello, my darling. Today I'll visit your house. When you're ready to leave, please tell me.' She dragged a grain of rice towards the hole. He crawled beside her. Hand in hand, they stood in the blinding sunlight. 'Hey, it's warmer out here.'

'Yes,' she answered.

When had he last seen the sun? No matter what happened, that golden medal would always be hanging above their heads. Dewy meadows, fresh air, the solitary stars. He couldn't believe it. He raised his joggling head exultingly.

PART THREE

I woke up in the middle of the night. A dull pain throbbed at the end of my spine. I hurried to the toilet and discovered that I was bleeding. Pain and blood? 'Mother, mother!' I rushed to my mother, shouting.

'What is it?'

'Mother, I'm bleeding.'

'Oh, that. You frightened me. I thought something horrible had hapened to you or to one of your brothers.'

'Mother, look at me,' I pleaded, pressing a towel between my legs.

'It's nothing really. You are a woman now.'

I looked at my thin legs and asked, 'A what?'

'A woman. Take one of the pads in my closet and use it.'

'Use it?' I was completely confused.

'To absorb the blood. This is what we call a period. You'll have it every month. Welcome to the community of women.'

'Me?' I noticed that my mother's hair was covered with the grey ashes of years. The fire had died out, leaving a dull grey substance. I asked her gently, 'Mother, why haven't you told me? You would have saved me all that trouble.' I snatched the pad and placed it between my legs. I felt so uncomfortable.

This thing would stay betwen my legs for one whole week. A bloody shadow was cast over my life. A woman! She must be joking.

I looked through the window at the brown mountains. The first threads of light appeared from somewhere behind the shadows. The birds disappeared from our sky. Who would like to hover over Al-Rabia' neighbourhood? No beautiful scenes around. I had no beauty whatsoever. I was sure that I was not a woman, because I had nothing in common with Um-Arrtin's customers. We were different species. 'You are a woman now,' my mother had said. The planets were kneaded together and the mountains were stuck to the sky, preventing the sun from squeezing itself out again. She reminded me of Sheikh Musa who preached on Friday. 'Damn the sinner. You are all atheists.' He used to cram his speech with 'h' sounds. 'The horrible, hörrendous hardship when God's hurricane hit human beings . . .' Forgive him God, he went astray.

Time to go to work. I hated that job, but it was better than nothing. Um-Arrtin was almost blind and could not see her needles. The only healthy thing was her tongue. I sewed, swept and sometimes cooked for that poor woman. I pulled the black dress over my head and noticed that it was tighter than before. 'My dear dress. If you'd been able to go to court, you would have complained. Don't worry. Um-Arrtin gave me a piece of cloth. I'll sew it and set you free.'

Omar, Bakir and Malik were asleep. The humming of their breath filled the air. Hanin, my aunt, who used the only bed in the room, was quiet too. Lately, Old Man Suffocation had begun visiting her. He wanted to strangle her, but instead left her breathless and shaking. 'Hanin, wake up.'

146

'What do you want?'

'I got my period today.'

'You little wretch. Be happy, your days of misery have started.'

Hanin was drivelling again. I saw one of Abeer's Tales on my pillow. 'The Black Villain'. Why didn't they write about periods? Handsome men meet reluctant women and fall in love with them. The periodless woman yields to the charm of the black villain who turns out to be perfect. I felt let down by my favourite tales.

I prepared breakfast for the family. Cheese, thyme and olive oil, bread and tea. I went through to my mother, who had turned into a few whitish bones pulled together by thin flesh, and kissed her hand. 'Good morning, mother.' In a wink, she had been whisked from youth to old age. After they murdered my father, she spent days crying and asking for him. My raging uncle said, 'No.' I would never forgive him for beating me up because I disobeyed him and went to the yard that day. He treated us as if we were soldiers in his regiment. That bloody uncle visited us once a year and claimed to be responsible for us.

'Good morning, Eman.' She pulled herself together and sat up in bed.

'Here's your breakfast, best looking mother in the world.'

She tightened the muscles of her face but never smiled. Never.

'Did you wake your brothers up?'

'Yes. They're having breakfast in the kitchen.'

She frowned and said, 'You are a woman now. Be careful.' Then she was gone to some other place, as if she was sick of this one.

I walked to the bus-stop and saw Shamma'eh in the way. My uncle would be angry if he saw me talking

147

even to Shamma'eh. That uncle of mine. 'Hi, gorgeous.' Since he had no teeth, his smile looked hollow and childish. 'Good morning *th*weet Eman', he lisped.

'You haven't got married yet?'

'I have ten and I need thirty more.'

'That will take a long time.'

'Ye*th*, what can I do?'

Poor Shamma'eh was shrinking in his trousers. The badly-built houses of the neighbourhood were sinking deep in mud and garbage. When they arrested my father, they arrested the smiles on our faces too. When they murdered him, they killed the joy in our hearts. Happiness must ask for a special pass to be allowed into the slums.

One day, my uncle yanked my hair and pushed me into our house. He threw me down on the floor and shouted, 'Look what your daughter has done!' I didn't know what he was talking about. 'She smiled at a young man on the bus.'

I shouted through tears, 'He offered me his seat so I thanked him and smiled. What's wrong with that?'

He slapped my face and roared, 'Slut.'

Me? Slut? The bastard. I spat in his face and screamed, 'Don't ever call me that.'

He threw me down on the floor and sat on top of me and started punching me with his fists. Blows hit me from all directions until I fainted. When I woke up, I was in my mother's bed. Um-Musaad wet my forehead with cold water, then wiped my face. She said under her breath, 'I wish I'd been here. I'd have wrenched his head off, that bastard brother of yours.'

'Eman, it's all right, love,' said Hanin. Her words brought on a fit of weeping. I just couldn't believe

what had happened. How dare he call me a slut?
Hanin kissed my forehead and said, 'I knew that
you'd eat shit every day of your life, love.' My
mother sat silently in her chair.

'Do you trust me? Will you believe it if I tell you
that I don't know that man?' They nodded their
heads collectively. 'Then why let him beat me like
that?'

'What can I do?' asked mother.

Um-Musaad clenched her fist. 'I wish I'd been
here.'

Hanin said, 'I was in the other room. When I heard
your voice, I ran and found him on top of you like a
monster on top of a dead pigeon.'

That night Hanin let me sleep in her bed and she
sat on the floor reading me some of Nizar Qabani's
poetry.

> 'They shake the tombs of saints,
> Hoping the tombs of saints will give them rice
>   and children.
> They spread out elegant soft carpets
> And amuse themselves with an opium we call
>   fate.
> And destiny
> In my country, in the country of the simple.'

She shook her head and said, 'If your uncle saw us
he'd kill us. Reading the poetry of that scoundrel,
he'd say.' I couldn't help it. I wanted a rich handsome man who would say, 'Will you marry me?' as
soon as he set eyes on me. He would kiss me with his
gentle lips and the stars would fall down to earth and
pile up in my palms. I shivered as if my head were
see-through, like chiffon, and what went on inside
was visible.

I eventually went to sleep and dreamt that I lived in a spacious palace like Uncle Amin's. Stairs, crystal chandeliers, gold handles, hot and cold water. Whenever I tried to undress in my Palace, a shabby beggar would break in. I pushed him out and closed the doors, but again more beggars appeared suddenly in front of me. I spent all night pushing the shabby figures out, afraid that their filthy feet would leave marks on the thick carpets.

The next morning I made sure that my brothers, my mother and Hanin had their breakfast and went to work. For some time now, Um-Arrtin's hands had been shaking with age, and more and more I was having to take over and run the place for her. 'What's that bruise?' she asked.

'I fell down,' I said. She knew that I was lying. Between me and her a strange bond had developed through the years. She supported me when Daddy was murdered by raising my salary to sixty dinars plus a dress every year in the festival. I tried to save five every month in order to pay the exam fees. Something inside pushed me towards education. Maybe because my father wanted me to finish school, or maybe because people called me the prisoner's daughter and avoided me as if I had alopecia. I didn't know.

On the way to the bus-stop I remembered Malik and smiled. I bought him the notebook and pencil he had asked for. If I bought some candies I would kiss good-bye the bus ride back home. I bought some sweets for Omar and Bakir, some fruits, and trudged back home.

The Democratic State of Israel – Beer Sheva – 1985

David parked his car in front of Arad synagogue, which had a candelabra exterior. It was modern, as modern as the Arad settlement. All it needed was candles to be lit and give out the light of the Torah. He tiptoed into the almost deserted building. The soles of his feet welcomed the cool marble. He filled his nostrils with the smell of olive wood – the low chairs surrounding the main hall and most of the partitions were made of it. He covered his head with the prayer-shawl and sat in the sanctuary. The silence and the flickering light of the candle seeped through his soul. He sighed, took the two wooden boxes containing the Torah verses, tied them to himself with the leather thongs and started reading:

'He that walketh righteously, and speaketh uprightly;
He that despiseth the gain of oppressions,
That shaketh clear his hands from laying hold on bribes,
That stoppeth his ears from hearing of blood
And shutteth his eyes from looking upon evil.'

'David,' whispered Rabbi Elijeh.
'Yes.'
'Are you all right?' he asked, inspecting him

through his tiny glasses.

The Rabbis know everything. You live to learn, but to what end?

'Yes, I have just finished the Resignation.'

'Cast your burden on the Lord.'

David shook his head and stared at the grey marble. Rabbi Elijeh ran his fingers over his bushy white beard and asked, 'What is bothering you? Tell me.'

'Nothing, really. I am just exhausted. So exhausted that I want to give up.'

'No son of this country will give up. Just adhere to your religion and you will be all right.' He looked at him with his penetrating eyes that miss nothing. 'Do you still work in the prison?'

'Yes.'

He nodded his head thoughtfully and said,' I know your illness, but I don't have the medicine.'

David fixed his eyes on the Ark of the Law. The pressure inside him increased. Give vent. Give vent.

Rabbi Elijeh walked to the pulpit and said, 'Centuries ago, the prophet Ezekiel said something in the name of the God of Israel. Look around you and you will realize that it was a prophecy. He said, "And that which cometh into your mind shall never come to pass; in that ye say: 'We shall be as the nations' . . . As I live, saith the Lord God, surely with a mighty hand and outstretched arm, and with fury outpoured, will I rule over you."'

'How can I stop my ears from hearing and shut my eyes?' he asked, and touched the grey marble with his hands. The candles fixed on the two ornamental chandeliers in the corners burnt themselves out right to the very end.

'The righteous shall live by his faith.'

The Rabbi's words echoed in the empty hall and clanged against the walls. He looked at the women's

152

gallery and saw Judith waving and smiling at him. Although the spacious place was cold, he felt hot as if locked in a furnace. He touched his forehead. High temperature – fever. He'd better hurry back home. He rushed out and looked at the building again. Yes, it was like a candelabra. Not enough windows to see the flickering candle-light. The carpets swam over the marble. An engraved handle of a wooden chair in the men's section. The curtain of the Ark of the Law was dark velvet. Instrumental music. Couldn't distinguish it. Incense burnt and gave off trails of white smoke. A strange scent that took you back to woods, forest, nature, God. He shook his head. Was he hallucinating?

'You look awful. What happened?' asked Jud when she saw him.

'Nothing, Jud.'

'Are you all right?'

'I feel a little bit tired.'

She took his hand and said, 'You have a fever. I will ring the doctor.'

He ran his fingers through his sticky hair and said, 'No. I want to go to sleep.' He threw himself on the bed. She pulled the sheets to cover him. Stupid woman. No. He flung them away. Her light eyes looked worried and he turned his head to the other side. The devil with his fork was standing over his head and blowing hot air. The room was boiling hot, the city, the desert. God damn the Negev. He tossed his head on the pillow and smiled when he remembered his Bar Mitzvah in Zawichest. His moustache was as fluffy as the hair on a cucumber. He put on his white shirt and white skullcap and walked proudly to the synagogue. The Rabbis tried to teach all the boys how to tie the leather thongs. One of these Bibles is next to your heart. He fixed it on his left arm. The next to your forehead then to your left arm. He entwined his fingers and whispered, 'I will betroth thee unto Me forever.' One of the boys got completely entangled in the straps and they laughed at him. Don't give me that baby. His head is loose, I might break his neck. 'Go on,' she said and handed him the baby. The head moved in a strange way as if not connected to the body. He pulled the embroidered bonnet and touched the fuzzy hair. 'What a lovely child.' With his fingers, he touched a lump and the baby began shrieking. He looked at the back of its head. 'What is that?' he asked the mother and almost threw the baby on the floor. A gaping burn covered with leeches. 'It's nothing really. Just a burn.' Some of the leeches crept down the tender body and he started shaking. 'Take him. Take him.' 'No, he's yours.' He laid him on his lap and began crying. Jud's voice?

'David, David, darling.' Her light eyes swam in front of him. Right behind her stood a white figure.

'Don't worry, Mrs. Dzentis. He'll be all right.'

She put a cold cloth on his forehead. Pleasant but stinging.

'Are you all right, darling?'' How could she ask him that question? She hadn't given him a child and still she asked that question, with her serene smile!

'Are you all right?' God damn it. He looked at her with bright eyes and said, 'No. I am not all right and don't ever ask me that stupid question.'

'David, darling.'

'Don't "darling" me, Jud. Saint Jud, cool Jud.'

She continued wetting his body with cold water. Nothing would make her angry. Nothing would force her to go away. If he was really sterile she would have left him ages ago. They lied to him. They all lied to him. He was a perfect man. He slipped his hand

154

under his pants and said to her shadow, 'I am a man. Look. I can bring new lives to this world.' Her blurred face disappeared and he heard the sound of suppressed weeping. He pressed his hands on his head and shouted, 'I love you. Forgive me.'

The devil suffocated him with his stinking breath. The leech crawled into his fluffy moustache. The Rabbi shook with laughter and his white beard danced. All the boys pointed at him and cracked with laughter. Bastards.

Yassin, the barber, proposed to Hanin. He visited us
with his mother and two other old women. I opened
the door for them and led them to the sitting room,
He had developed a belly and his lumpy shoulders
were still sprinkled with dandruff. Two thin strands
of hair, pushed from behind his ears upwards, covered his bald head. Mother pulled herself from the
bed and sat with them. 'Ask Hanin to come.'

I went to bring her from the bedroom. She was
curled on top of the bed, weeping. 'Why are you
crying?'

'I hate that man.'

'Then say no.'

'Life is much more complicated than you think.'
She cupped her face with her hands. Time had
loosened the skin around her bones and left her with
sagging cheeks. She had stopped wearing make-up
after they murdered my father. She spent most of her
time on that bed as if stitched to it. Although I had
vowed not to love anybody, something inside me
stirred when I saw her that day.

I went to the sitting rom. The old women behaved
so arrogantly. Each of their movements said, 'We are
doing you a favour by proposing to this daughter of
yours.' I said loudly, 'She doesn't want to see you.'

'Please, Um-Eman, let me talk to her,' Yassin

begged my mother.

'Yes, Eman, go with him.' Of course, a man alone in our bedroom. It would be a scandal.

'Hanin,' he pleaded.

'What are you doing here?' she said and tidied her half-blonde, half-grey hair.

'God only knows how difficult it was for me to convince my mother to come. It took me a couple of years. She's here. Please come and see her. I want you to be my wife.'

Hanin eyed him and started crying again. He was not exactly a knight riding his white horse. She nodded and he went back to the sitting room.

I overheard the old ladies blaming my mother for not thinking of marriage again. My mother said, 'What's left of my years is not as long as what has passed. God bring a good end.' I was angry. These old bitches. If my mother left us, we would have nobody to turn to. Nobody. Me and my three growing brothers.

I wondered what Hanin was doing. I went back and took her hand and led her to the sink. She washed her face and looked at the mirror.

'Look at my hair.'

'It's fashionable to tie a scarf around your head. I have one. I'll lend it to you. And please take off that stupid dress. You have plenty of other things.'

'Eman, do you want me to wear a mini-skirt again?'

'Yassin would love it.'

'Naughty kid.'

'Look, my father gave my mother an embroidered kaftan. She swore not to let the material touch her skin. You might as well use it. My father would be happy if his sister put it on.'

When Hanin traipsed into the room, Yassin's eyes gleamed with delight. That man loved her.

157

'Welcome our bride,' Yassin's mother said pompously, weighing Hanin up like a sheep she wanted to buy for the festival. Hanin shrank into one of the chairs. Her eyes swam dreamily in her doughy face.

'We have come here today to ask you for the hand of your daughter. What do you think, Um-Eman?'

'Hanin has nobody in the world who's responsible for her, except maybe my brother. I'll ask him and the first and last word will be his.'

Yes, mother. That brother of yours who got married and disappeared in his wife's bosom is responsible for our necks. Tell them. Go on. He bestowed his presence upon us in order to give us some drops of punishment because we were three women living alone in that house. The great veteran would never forgive us for that. Would he?

Hanin spent that night crying. The sad suppressed sound escaping from her lips mingled with the noises of the night. It was like a cough, a baby crying or a dog barking in the distance. I would never forget it.

'Hanin, if you don't want him, you should say no.'

She wiped her face with her flannel sleeve and said, 'The problem is more complicated.'

'What happened?'

'I'll tell you. I don't want you to make the same mistake. Do you remember the man who took us for a drive?'

'Yes, the prosecutor.'

'Mixed feelings drew me to him. First, he had my brother's fate in his hands, or so I thought. Second, he was good-looking. So, when he asked me to go with him for a drive, I accepted. After that a lot of things happened. I wanted him to help your father. I offered him my body. Thinking about it, maybe it was physical attraction and not a sacrifice. I really don't know. I went to his house that night and many

158

other nights. I lost my virginity and he betrayed me that day in the court.'

'What? You're not a virgin?' I said and pressed my hand to my stomach. Pain struck me as if someone had hit me.

'No, I'm not.'

'How can you get married to Yassin? As soon as he discovers that he'll throw you out.'

'Yassin knows about it. I told him when he dragged me out of the court. I think he loves me.'

'What?'

'Women always do that. It never works. Some get pregnant and suffer because of that.'

I remembered Nizar's poem:

'Don't turn pale,
It's only a hurried word:
I feel that I am pregnant.
You shouted out as if you had been stung,
"No, we'll tear the child apart".'

'Eman, don't ever commit this mistake. Our men have an old oriental fixation on virginity.'

'Don't worry. I'll never fall in love,' I said stretching my arms.

'Yassin loves me. That's why he accepted a second-hand woman. Since I am growing old, I'll accept him. He's my last chance. But what hurts my heart, what makes it smoulder, is the fact that *he* loves me and not anybody else. Why him? Why not somebody else?' She began to cry. 'Look at us. Poor, miserable outcasts. Sixteen heroes were forgotten in three years. What do you call us? What do you call this country?'

My eyelids hurt but I was determined not to cry. I was on my own and it was up to me to modify the rules of the game. I had made an iron rule: No love, no crying. I wanted to change the subject. 'What is taboo and what is not?'

'Taboo? Everything is taboo. Talking to men, looking at them, touching them. Anything that has to do with them. Don't ever succumb, love. Men like us to be hard to get. Don't ever yield.'

'Don't worry.' Society had torn at my poor aunt and chewed her up. Then it spat on the wreckage.

'Why Yassin?' she said and started crying again.

'Maybe he'll turn out to be a good husband.'

'They say he is mean. He keeps repairing his worn-out shoes.'

After a long day, I sighed and pushed the door open with my leg and put the sacks of fruit on the kitchen table. My brothers gathered around me like bees, so I gave Malik his share of sweets, then Omar, then Bakir. My mother was sitting in her chair staring at the brown mountains. The high peaks encircled the neighbourhood, isolating it from the rest of the world. She and the mountains had developed a bond between them through the years. Blood ties. No separation. Her body was withering away gradually. I feared that one day I would look at that damn chair and find it empty. I kissed her hand and said, 'Hello, mother.' She lowered her head. 'I brought you something you really like, apricot.' She moved her head. I wanted to bring her to life again but didn't know how.

She couldn't go to the factory after the disaster that struck us simply because she was too weak to stand up on her feet. All her beloveds were burnt out in front of her eyes and she couldn't do anything to save them. I was determined to take the exam for her and my father's sake. Thirty dinars would be enough for the fees and some books. I would try to borrow the rest from Sammah, who wanted to take the exam too. We decided to split the expenses between us. I planned to tell my mother that evening. So, after washing up the dishes I sat on the floor, leaning against her legs. 'Mother, I'll do the exam this year. I saved some money. I'll split the expenses between me and Sammah.' She moved in her chair.

'I promise that I'll pass and be a school teacher as you always wanted.' She rocked the chair. 'What more do you want?' She looked at me. Really looked at me for the first time in years. I laughed and said, 'All for you, Madam.'

She touched my hair with bony fingers and said, 'May God help you and give you happiness.'

'Just smile and eat properly and I'll be happy.'

'Oh, Eman, when I would rather be dead, how can you expect me to smile? When I keep praying to God to take my life in order to see your father and sister, how can I smile? Eman, I can't see the mountains now. I just see two faces on the horizon. Oh, Eman, your father was a good man who wanted to help poor people. And the presents he gave me! "Guess what I brought you, Alia?" he would say. He would always hide the gift behind his back and wait for my answer like a little child. Most of the time I knew what he had brought me, but I would not say. A bottle of perfume, a brooch, a kaftan. Each month had its own surprise. He was strict, yes. I didn't care, because I was happy to live with him in this house, give him children and feed them all. I was content. What killed your sister is what your father had been fighting. When she died I understood what your father did.'

I couldn't believe my ears. She was talking to me. 'Tell me more about him.'

'He believed that women were supposed to stay in the house, but all the same the neighbours called him the ally of women. Whenever a woman was beaten, he would support her against her brother or husband.'

'So, if he was alive he wouldn't have approved of what your brother did.'

'No, he wouldn't.' I jumped up, washed two apricots and threw one to her. She began to nibble at it.

Three weeks later, my brothers dashed into the room crying, 'My aunt, my aunt.' They stood in a line in front of Hanin. They were excited but uncomfortable in their new clothes. I turned over Malik's collar and combed his wet hair. Hanin looked at them with pride and said, 'It's true that he who has successors never dies.' She smiled to the beaming faces and said, 'Out, the bride wants to change.' They rushed out together as if they were one.

'He bought them the clothes I asked for.'

'Yes he did. Has he passed the test?'

I helped her to make up her face because her hands were shaking. She looked quite nice that day. 'I hope that Yassin will be a good husband. You deserve a good man.'

She hugged me and said, 'You deserve a good man too.' Hanin was plump and fair and I was thin and dark. She had dyed her hair and set it in the sixties style. I had a haircut that gave me a savage look. Each strand was a different length. I put on a blue dress. The edges were pleated as if I could fly away in it. My legs looked so thin in my mother's shoes.

I took Hanin's hand and we went into the sitting room. It was almost full. Um-Musaad served Cola to the guests. Yassin's mother and her two friends were talking loudly to each other. My brothers chased each other and my mother watched them, smiling. Um-Arrtin and Um-Tal'at were talking about America. My uncle's wife looked hot and bored. Shamma'eh was dancing in the middle. My friend Sammah was late.

Yassin smiled from the depth of his heart when he saw Hanin. She managed a smile and sat next to him on the sofa. The suit he was wearing was fading black. Time had spread the suit on the ground, then eaten and drunk sitting on it. Strands of hair were combed over his head. Shamma'eh and Um-Musaad began drumming and singing:

> 'Hey, mother of the bridegroom, God bless you.
> But if you don't dance we will not forgive you.'

My friend Sammah arrived and I ran to welcome her. 'Eman, you look beautiful.'

'You look beautiful too.' She was wearing her Palestinian dress. She lived next to Um-Arrtin's house, in a refugee camp. She sat next to Um-Musaad and joined in.

> 'Where are the horses
> That slash the night
> And carry me to my loved one's dwelling?'

My mother left the room suddenly. I knew what would happen so I followed her to the kitchen. She was leaning on the sink and crying like a baby. Her black dress shook as if nothing was inside it. I hugged her and said, 'Please don't spoil Hanin's wedding.'

'I just saw him sitting there. I swear to God that I saw him. And Amal was in his lap.'

163

'Please wash your face and go back.' I helped her wash and sent her back in. My bloody legs were shaking so much that I collapsed onto my mother's chair. The lights of the slums of Rahmah went out one by one. If only I could be born again, into a different life . . . Sammah touched my shoulder and said, 'We missed you.'

'I'm coming.'

Yassin gave Hanin a gold necklace, bracelet and ring. His face gleamed with joy as if he owned the earth and everything that was on it. With all the pride of a man who had got what he wanted, he buckled the bracelet around Hanin's wrist. Um-Musaad cried, 'Ya Ya Ya Ya.' Yassin took his bride's hand and walked through the door. All the women sang together:

> 'Hey Yassin, you're like a jasmine
> Your family is large!
> You're tall and handsome!
> Your aunts are singing for you
> Ya Ya Ya Ya
> We'll offer you something
> Worth more than gold.
> Ya Ya Ya Ya'

'It's getting cold. Let's go back to the nest,' he said to her. They crawled back to his nest. 'We might find some food there.'

'Yes,' she whispered.

'Fantastic walk. We'll do it again. What do you think?'

'It's fine with me.'

They squeezed themselves into the narrow passage. 'Here you are. Some grains.' She picked one up with her jaws.

'I won't be long.'

He wished that they wouldn't dig out his nest and step on him. He shuddered and lay down silently. If they didn't discover his hiding-place they might not step on him.

He couldn't understand why these children were still after him. Why couldn't they see that he was just a helpless tiny creature? They pointed at him with their deformed limbs and cracked with laughter. He crawled back to his nest. He dug it under the blazing sands of the desert, but the soil there was cold. He searched for that nice spot for hours. He dragged up some hay and covered the opening. 'Heh, heh.' He had beaten them all. He would stay there motionless for as long as it took. No fighting, killing, pain. 'Heh, heh.' The cold sands shrouded his body. Tickled him.

He wished they would not step on him. His jaws moved swiftly, grinding down grains. He would save some for winter, not like the stupid cicada. He said to him, while he was chirping shrilly in summer, 'While you were singing, I was collecting grains, lazybones. Since you have sung all summer, you can eat shit now.'

The giant creatures entered the nest. Trespassing. How in hell had they squeezed themselves down the passage? 'Out, out, shitty dogs,' he hissed. They had tall legs, as tall as palm trees. He wished that they would leave him alone. He raised his joggling head and winked at them. Two small faces on both ends of a cloud in the shape of a triangle. A white patch that was stamped inside his eye.

'You're being transferred to the wards. Let's go.'

He stood firmly on all six legs, stretched his feelers and opened his jaws. 'No'.

'Please come with us.'

'If you don't leave me alone I'll sting you. It's poisonous.' They laughed.

'It's poisonous,' he said. He pointed at his head. 'The bird has flown away. Come on, kid, let's go.' He crawled back to the corner. The foggy faces grew bigger. 'Leave me alone.' He shut his bulging eyes firmly so as not to see them step on him. They would break his joints and flatten his head and belly. 'No, No!' he shouted. Kill. Kill. Slash with your scout's knife. Open your jaws wide and show them your teeth. His body jerked when he realized that they would step on him at any moment. His head exploded and he attacked them with all his strength. Ready to strike, stab, kill.

'I think we need the doctor's help. Go quickly.'

He raised his right leg and tried to shield his face. 'Mmm,' he stammered and lowered his head.

'Hey, don't be afraid. We'll take you to a better place.'

He had never seen a two-legged monster before. Mmm. Where had she gone? She might have helped him get rid of them. He wished she would come back.

'Where are you? Help me please.'

A prick – and the passages of the nest collapsed on his head like an avalanche. Soil and more soil until he was sure that they had killed him. He lay in his own grave. His six legs were flattened against the ground and his feelers were paralyzed. Shit. He shivered when he found himself in the abyss. Shrieks? Echoes?

'My sister, he came back yesterday wearing a hat and shorts,' said Um-Musaad.

'What? Tal'at wearing shorts?' said my mother.

Impossible. My heart jerked in my chest. My best friend Tal'at had returned. When? Why? I cleared my throat and asked, 'When?'

'Yesterday. But, I tell you, he's not an Arab any more. He's a Mister now.' Um-Musaad hit her breast with her hand and added, 'We live and learn.'

The boy who used to sit on the doorstep fiddling with that hopeless bicycle – he'd grown into a Mister? When we cooked petals in cans, he used to be the father and collected sticks for us. When Rida was on fire, I didn't know what to do or who to call for help. I mised her badly. The even colours of the maps Tal'at used to draw for me baffled my classmates. He promised that my father would come back from prison. Now, he would never come back. How could I forgive him for that? He deserted me, left me alone to face the gushing wind of misfortune. The scent of the jasmine necklace he used to make me filled our bedroom for days. How could I forget the games we played together? I must see him. With trembling hands, I pulled the blue dress over my head, then brushed my hair. 'Mother, I am going to Um-Tal'at's house.'

'Don't be late.'

I noticed that Um-Musaad winked at my mother. That woman. Tal'at would be a man. Different? What would he look like after all these years? I knocked on their door and said, 'Hello.'

'Welcome, Eman. We haven't seen you for ages,' said Um-Tal'at, and fixed the wire frame of her glasses behind her ears with shaking hands.

I clasped my hands and said, 'It's my work.'

'God bless you.'

Tal'at came into the room. At first, I couldn't look at him, then I raised my head. The years that had passed stretched between us and we stood there like strangers. I caught a glimpse of the shorts Um-Musaad was going on about all morning. His dark legs were firmer and taller. Gosh, the thin Tal'at had vanished and in his place stood that dark, tall man.

'Hi, baby,' he greeted me in English and sat down without shaking my outstretched hand. I sat opposite him on the sofa.

'Welcome back,' I said.

He looked me over, then said, 'You've changed.' His eyes had something I didn't understand and didn't like.

'You've changed too.' I wanted the conversation to keep going.

'Of course I have. America – America is marvellous – everything is so exciting. The cars. The fertility – it's so green! The technology. Really advanced – not like this stinking neighbourhood.'

At that very moment, I discovered how much I loved my country and the 'stinking neighbourhood' he was talking about. My cheeks became blazing hot as if Tal'at had slapped me on the face.

'What irritated me when I went down the steps of the airplane was the dust. This fucking place is dry and white like a tomb.'

'Er – how many years have you spent there?'

'About five. Why?'

'Because listening to you, anybody would think that you had been born there.'

He smiled apologetically. I wished that he hadn't come back. I wished that he wouldn't spoil the mental picture I'd kept of him. A smiling boy sitting on the doorstep.

'Eman, you're still thin and fiery-tempered.'

'Not like American women, of course.'

He took my remark seriously and said, 'Not at all, no. Most of them are blonde. Very fit too. They go for sports a lot.'

'I assume that they have a place to play sports in.'

'Yes, a lot of sports centres and parks. Not like this dirty neighbourhood. Bloody hell, even people are so lazy and dirty.'

As one of the dirty people he was insulting, I was not pleased at all. The 'voice of America' didn't belong to our neighbourhood.

He scratched his balls and went on sprinkling his jewels, 'But still our women are purer, virgins, not sleep-and-run.' He laughed at his Anglo-Arab joke, then switched on the record-player. 'I brought it with me. I bought it for 200 dollars.'

The only time I saw a dollar note was when a tourist tried to convince a salesman in the antiques market to take dollars instead of dinars. The salesman shook his head and said no to the bunch of outstretched notes. I really admired him for that.

'Can you understand what he's saying?' The singer kept repeating one syllable, 'Da Da Da – Da Da Da.'

'Of course not. How could I?'

He stood up and began revolving. 'Excuse me, I must go.' He nodded while repeating with the singer, 'Da Da Da – Da Da Da.'

America for me was tanned women in backless blouses walking hand in hand with men in the market place of Rahmah. Once, in an old copy of *Home and Garden*, I saw a picture of a garden full of bright yellow daffodils.

'What do you think?' asked Um-Musaad, when she saw me.

'He's not the Tal'at I know.'

'God punish the westerns. They take our young men, corrupt them, then throw them back to us soft in the head.'

Tal'at was not soft in the head. He prefered virgins. Hanin was not a virgin, but all the same, there was nothing wrong with her. She got married too. Mind you, she used to complain a lot of Old Father Suffocation.

The next day, Tal'at came to visit us with his mother. I welcomed them and led them to the sitting room. 'Mother, I wonder what brought them here tonight?

'We shall see.'

Our kitchen was in a mess, so I attacked it with an enthusiasm that surprised me. Fifteen minutes later, the cooker was spotless, the plates and pots and pans were washed and dried and even the cupboard was sparkling. My mother came towards me smiling. There must be something wrong.

'Tal'at has just asked me for your hand. He wants to marry you and take you to America with him.' To America, America where everything was so marvellous and exciting.

I asked my mother earnestly, 'What do you honestly think of him?'

'I don't know. Anyway, it's your decision.'

171

In our neighbourhood poverty and humiliation were the sultans. Tal'at had opened a door for me to escape the misery. Yet if I left Malik, Omar, Bakir and my mother, who would take care of them? To live in the country of green grass and yellow daffodils? I went to the sitting room with the apron around my waist.

'Hi, baby,' he said in English. He had forgotten our language.

'How are you,' I said in standard Arabic. His mother and mine left the room quietly.

'Not too bad. Eman, I would like to take you with me. Show you the world. A pretty girl like you deserves a better place than this.'

A pretty girl like me? A kind of satisfaction blossomed inside me, as if nourished by his sweet words. Just listening to these words was so pleasing.

'This area stinks. We'll live in a clean place.'

Whenever he referred to my neighbourhood in that way, I couldn't help feeling offended. Anger had beaten satisfaction inside me. I pushed my hair away from my face and bit my lip. No. If Shamma'eh was garbage, I was garbage too. I would spend my life in that place with my family in the dirt. Why? I didn't know. How was I going to explain it to Tal'at?

'I want to continue my studies.'

'Why?' he said. When he saw my expression, he added quickly, 'If you insist you can do that there.'

'In Arabic?' I was sounding like Al-Khalil Ibn-Ahmmad, the father of the Arabic language. I laughed and this encouraged him to ask again, 'Eman, will you marry me?'

'Why don't you get married to one of the white-skinned women?'

172

'I wouldn't marry a woman I have eaten,' he said indignantly.

'Eaten?'

'Slept with.'

At that point, I became dead sure that Tal'at was not for me. He somehow reminded me of my uncle. Also, miles and miles spread between us. He hadn't seen my father being hanged. He hadn't been here when my aunt had a nervous breakdown. My mother didn't open her mouth for one whole week. He would never understand what I had been through, what the neighbourhood had been through.

'No, Tal'at. My answer is no.'

My answer surprised and confused him. A typical reaction of an outsider. We definitely didn't suit each other. Well, if you add cardamom to instant coffee or hot spices to hamburger, the taste is bound to be funny.

David put the bag in the car boot and said to Jud, 'A good idea. We'll enjoy this weekend with the Nissims.' She tied a scarf around her neck and nodded. A surge of love moved him towards her. Touch her. 'Jud, let me fix the scarf.' He kissed her. 'Thanks for your support, love. I gave you a hard time when I was ill.'

She smiled and said, 'If we don't start we'll never get there.'

As they drove off he said, 'We haven't seen them for quite some time.'

'You ignored all their invitations.'

'It's a long drive.' Nisanit and Jacob, the Nissims' children, were so lovely. Nisanit's long blonde hair was as smooth as silk. Her mother always put two flowers at the sides to push it away from her rounded face. Their son, Jacob, had the answers to any question. David felt the warmth of Jud's hand on his and smiled.

'You know, Dav, you've lost some weight.'

'Really?' he said, looking down at his belly.

'You look better.'

'Thanks, madam. You are as fit as ever.' He wished she was not that slim. 'I went to the synagogue last week, and because of that I fell ill.' They both laughed.

174

'Dav, I have a feeling that something is bothering you.'

'No. Just exhaustion.'

They reached Tel Aviv – Gaza crossing. 'Welcome to the Hawaii of Israel.'

She laughed and said, 'It's better than Hawaii.'

A group of teenage boys surrounded the car. David had to stop. 'What do they want?'

'Please, sir, give us work – whatever wage you like,' they shouted.

'Hey, I'm not looking for workers, I'm on holiday. It's getting dark. Why don't you give up?'

The tired faces stared at him with a fixed expression. 'Excuse me.' He pressed the horn and moved. 'They are still waiting for someone to pick them up.'

'Those Arabs. They'll frighten off the tourists.'

'We're getting closer to the sea. I can smell it.'

'Darling, stop here. I want to have a look.'

He parked the car and they stood near the shore. He stretched his arms and said, 'The fresh air! It's so salty.' Jud took off her sandals and worked her toes into the sands. 'Careful.' She ran like an excited child. He felt she would melt away, that he wouldn't be able to touch her again.

'Where are you off to? You'll never get away from me.'

He picked her up and carried her and she laughed. He hadn't heard that sweet sound for quite a while.

'Let's go.' They took a narrow road that left the sea behind. On an iron gate 'The plantation of Yahuda Nissim' was written in white. An old Arab guard opened it and asked, 'Who are you?'

'My name is David Dzentis.'

The guard closed the gate and a few seconds later came back and said, 'Welcome, Mr. Dzentis.' David slowed down. The road was not paved and the only sign of human occupation was the tracks of the tractor wheels. It was lined with citrus trees, heavy with their orange and lemon. The leaves' green colour looked even lighter when mingled with the orange and yellow.

'Oh, what a lovely smell!' said Jud.

'There must be a canal somewhere. I can hear the water streaming.'

An old building appeared behind the trees. He parked the car near the canal that surrounded it. Yahuda and Leha crossed the footbridge to welcome them.

'Hello, my friend.'

'Hello, Yahuda, Leha.'

'Judith.' He kissed her cheek.

'What a lovely place!'

'Please, come in.' His teeth gleamed when he smiled. He looked happy and damned healthy. 'Judith, you look great.'

They sat on the verandah on straw chairs. The dusk made the citrus trees look taller and the sound of running water louder. 'Yahuda, this is marvellous.'

'Yes, but expensive to run.' He crossed his legs and David noticed that he was wearing expensive clothes and white shoes. White?

The next morning, Jud took David's hand and said, 'Let's go to the beach. It's not far.'

'Jud, it's early.'

'No, it's not, spoiled kid. Come on, move it!'

'All right, all right.' They took their towels and ran to the beach. The sun barely touched the water. The waves foamed along their feet. 'Ladies first.'

'No, after you.'

'Together, then?'

'Yes, together.' They held hands and walked slowly into the water. His legs were ticklish. He smiled. 'Come on,' he said and splashed her with cold water.

176

'You beast,' she shouted and plunged his head into the water. He floated on his back, closing his eyes. The sun became warmer. He would never think about that bastard again. The nightmare wouldn't spoil his life. If he couldn't have children, he could at least have peace of mind. He could travel easily. No worrying. Where they were or what they were doing. My son is dumb and my daughter is ugly. He opened his eyes. Silver for seconds, then the colours crept back to the scene. Mostly blue and white. When he swam back, Jud was drying her hair.

The sands were almost white, and so pure. He saw an Arab squatting near the water. A fisherman because he was wearing wide black trousers, a white shirt and a tight woollen hat. His eyes searched the horizon. 'Are you looking for something?' David asked him. The man eyed him, then stared at the water. 'Have you lost something?' He took a handful of soil and toyed with it. His trousers were streaked all over with dried salt from hundreds of days at sea. He stood up, looked at them, spat on the sand and walked away.

'Why did he do that?'

'Darling, you know Arabs. It's one of their habits.'

They carried the towels and jogged back to the plantation. The old guard opened the gate and let them in. 'He didn't like seeing you in the bikini.'

'Women should be wrapped in hundreds of layers to turn Arab men on.'

David was still laughing when he caught sight of Nisanit and Jacob. Their tiny feet were dangling in the water. 'Hello, uncle. Hello, aunt,' they waved to them.

'Hello.' Nisanit's hair was tied with flowers and Jacob was leaner and taller than he remembered. Nisanit ran to David and said. 'Please, carry me

177

back.' Jacob looked at Jud's legs and said, 'You have a lovely figure, aunt.' David hemmed and Jacob smiled.

'I can smell fish,' Nisanit complained.

'Of course. I was swimming with the fish.'

Jacob asked Jud, 'Were you swimming too?' That boy was not too far from his Bar Mitzvah.

They took a shower and joined their hosts. Coffee was being served. Yahuda gazed at his face and said, 'Days pass like a mirage. I remember your wedding as if it took place yesterday. We celebrated in the kibbutz. Remember?' He waved his hands in the air and recited,

'The days of Youth like clouds of smoke will pass.
Ere evening falls thou shalt be withered grass
Though morning saw thee like a lily blow.'

'Solomon Ibn Gabirol,' said Jud.

'Yes, dear,' Yahuda said. 'Talking of lilies, I am trying to plant some water lilies in the small pool behind the house. White. The only memory of my birth-place I brought to Israel.'

Leha said, 'Excuse me,' and called the children. 'Please come back and drink your juice and take your vitamins.' She looked at Jud and said, 'Kids!', as if raising them meant running the whole world.

'I know,' said Jud, 'I teach in a kindergarten. Remember?'

'Enjoy the Sabbath.'

'She will stay with the kids,' said Yahuda and smiled. Dazzling teeth. Yahuda seemed to David happy, fit and rich. 'I will take you for a walk around the plantation. I am building an artificial lake to irrigate the trees and raise fish.'

'It's a good idea, but it must be expensive.'

'Actually, it is. Mind you, manpower is so cheap.'
'Let Mohammad do it?'
'Yes, Arab hands.'

They walked along a footpath, ducking their heads to avoid low branches. 'It's a good year,' remarked Yahuda.

They stood near an excavation. 'This is the lake. The constructor promised to finish it next month.' Cement sacks, iron bars and a lot of dug-out soil. It will make the place different.'

'You mean ugly.'

'It's profitable.'

He saw an Arab leaning on the sacks. He was wearing a white head-dress and a white kaftan lined with black. He put his finger on his lips to silence them because the old man was singing.

'Do you have sailors, captain?
Dark and oriental, captain?
Take us to our country, captain,
To smell it's soil, captain.'

'Hello, Hajj.' He nodded his head. 'You have a beautiful voice.'

'My son, I used to sing at weddings.'

'Please, Hajj, some more.'

He looked at the setting sun and said,

'Night: let the captive finish his song;
By dawn his wing shall flutter
And the hanged one will swing in the wind.'

When he started singing his voice was weak and rusty, but when he moved to the second stanza it became stronger and sharper:

179

'Night: slow your pace,
Let me pour out my heart to you;
Perhaps you forget who I am
And what my troubles are.
Pity how my hours have slipped
Through your hands;
Do not think I weep from fear,
My tears are for my country . . .'

With the end of his brownish sleeve, he wiped his tears.

'He is as strong as fifty workers, but a bit sentimental. Always crying.'

'Typical,' said Jud and winked at him.

He gazed at her and said, 'Let's go back.'

They went into the dining rom. Leha had done a wonderful job. The table was set with china, crystal, silver chandeliers. The candle-light flickered in the gentle breeze. The smell of incense and citrus filled the whole plantation and spread as far as the sea. They started eating and drinking wine.

'Ophra washeth her garments in the waters of
    my tears,
And spreadeth them out in the sunshine of her
    radiance.
She demandeth no water of the fountains,
    having my two eyes,
And no other sunshine than her beauty.'

'Is that Hajj always crying?'

Yahuda looked irritated and said, 'I'll tell you something you won't believe. That Hajj is the previous owner of this place. He couldn't prove his ownership, so I paid him some compensation and offered him a job. He said that he'd spent most of his life digging this soil so he might as well go on doing it.'

'Amazing.'

'All right, Yahuda, but he wouldn't have modernized the place,' Leha said.

'He resents the change.'

'They're all lazy and unimaginative.'

Jacob tried to stay silent, then he said suddenly, 'These asses should all be killed.'

'Horrible,' objected his mother.

'Who told you that?' David asked.

'We agreed upon that in the school. We don't want dirty people in our country.'

'But, Jasmine, Hajj Mohammad's daughter, is clean and beautiful. She's my friend. Please Jacob, don't kill her.'

'For you, I won't.'

They all laughed, but David stopped eating and said, 'Excuse me. I'm really tired and I would like to get some sleep.'

'I'll join you, Dav.'

'It's been a wonderful weekend.'

'We're very glad you came.'

'Goodnight,' he said, and kissed Nisanit's forehead. She giggled.

In the bedroom, Jud said, 'Something upset you downstairs. You didn't finish eating.'

'Nothing. My migraine.'

'Your migraine?' She brought a glass of water and his tablets. 'Dav, my hand is always stretched to you. Take it whenever you feel like it.'

'Do you mind if I keep the curtains open? I want to see the full moon.'

'Yes, love.' He threw himself on the bed. 'Yahuda reminded me of our wedding.'

'Your hands were shaking when you threw the glass,' she said and took off her robe.

'All those people were looking at me. My Hebrew wasn't that good. I almost blew it with the Rabbi.' Jud laughed. David looked at the moon. Smouldering fire. Almost covering the whole sky.

'I'll never forget the carriage your friends decorated.'

'A seat pulled by a tractor.'

'The olive branches were hissing like arrows over our heads.'

'We were all drunk.' Her gentle features were almost transparent under the moonlight. She stretched her hand to him and he took it.

'Jud, the next few days will be hard. Will you support me?'

'Of course.'

'Even if I do something that others might consider strange?'

'What are you going to do, for God's sake?'

'Quit my job.'

'What? Why?'

'I'm getting old and I want to spend my last days peacefuly in one of the agricultural kibbutzim. Plant, plough, eat and read the Torah.'

'But your job is well-paid.'

'It's exhausting. And all my colleagues were promoted except me. I don't want their bloody promotion.'

'Is this the real reason?'

'I don't know what the exact reason is, but I've made up my mind.'

'What makes you happy, makes me happy too.'

Jud was giving and forgiving. Why live with a sterile man? Love? Maybe.

'Your face glows in the moonlight.'

'You have a sexy figure,' she said and ran her tongue over her lips.

'Oh, really,' he said, raising his hands and exposing his teeth. She screamed and he fell on top of her. 'Your neck.' He kissed her warm skin. 'Dav,' she whispered, 'I know that what is bothering you has to do with Arabs. I will always be by your side.'

'You'd better be or I'll bite you.'

'No, have mercy, Dracula!'

He kissed her. He was a healthy man. Nothing was wrong with him. He felt it.

The next morning they said good-bye to the Nissims and drove back to Beer Sheva. Jud waved her scarf. 'Bye-bye, Hawaii.'

At the crossing David blew the horn and the Arab kids opened a way for him to pass. Despair incarnate. He looked back at them and waved to them. Jud was going to object, but she bit her lip.

The Democratic State of Ishmael – Rahmah – 1980

We decided to pay Hanin, or Mrs. Khashab, a visit.
After discussing what we could afford, we bought her
a small carpet as a present and shared the expenses
with Um-Musaad. So, on Friday, Malik, Bakir and
Omar wore the clothes Yassin had bought them. I
put on one of my mother's skirts and a T-shirt. My
mother looked grim in her black cape and veil.
Um-Musaad marched in front, carrying the carpet
under her arm. We took the bus to the Harim's
Alley. My brothers were so excited because that visit
was their first outing. They ran after each other in the
bus, then squeezed their faces at one window. 'God,
look at that car!' said Bakir. A halo of silence circled
my mother. 'I hope she's happy or else I'll wrench
her husband's head off,' said Um-Musaad.

'If you always did what you threatened, we'd be
living among headless neighbours!'

She smiled and said, 'You know, it took three men
to save that lawyer from me. I was literally going to
wrench his head off. Believe me.'

'We're there,' I said to my mother and we walked
along the alley until we reached a high building. The
houses were set on top of each other randomly, as if
they had been poured into the narrow space from a
cement-mixer. 'She lives on the third floor.' We went
up the stairs and rang the bell. Hanin opened the

door. Yassin was standing right behind her. Her hair was tied with a pink ribbon and the satin navy-blue kaftan she was wearing emphasized the whiteness of her skin. She seemed happy enough.

'Please come in,' she said. We kissed, shook hands and hugged.

'We missed you,' my mother said.

'I missed the three *afreets* very much,' she said and hugged them one by one.

The flat consisted of a bedroom, a kitchen and a sitting room. Not bad.

Yassin said, 'I'll buy some bread. I won't be long.'

As soon as he was out of earshot, Um-Musaad asked, 'Is he good to you?'

Hanin laughed. 'He is kind and understanding. I say "Yes" to everything he says, but I get whatever I want indirectly.'

'Wise woman, not like Eman – she'll blacken our faces one day.'

'What's wrong with me?' I asked indignantly.

'You will throw the truth into your husband's face and nobody likes that.'

'I told you. I won't get married.'

We sat around the table and ate what Hanin had cooked. The stuffed chicken glowed and gave off the aroma of mixed spices. She admitted that Yassin had helped her, but he insisted that she was the one who deserved all the compliments. My mother said unexpectedly, 'Brother-in-law, could you help me find a way to get back the shop from Sami? His claims are groundless and can be proved illegal. Mahmud's spirit dwells in that shop.'

'Of course, Um-Eman, I'll do whatever you need.'

'Please, talk to Sami and try to work something out.'

'All right, I will.'

185

So after all these years, my mother was still thinking about the bookshop. I thought she had forgotten about that crook.

'Hey, kids, would you like some sweets?' The boys ran after Hanin to the kitchen.

'Bright kids, Um-Eman, God protect them,' said Yassin.

'It's your turn, Yassin. Tighten your belt and make that woman pregnant,' said Um-Musaad.

'Don't start,' Hanin shouted from the kitchen.

Um-Musaad looked him in the eye and said, 'That woman has suffered a lot in her life. Please be kind to her. Now you are her father, brother and husband. It's a big responsibility to shoulder.'

'Hanin is as dear to me as my eyesight. Don't worry, Um-Musaad.'

Hanin entered the room. Her cheeks were flushed and she was laughing because she had saved the harisah tray from my brothers. They came running in and she raised the tray high. 'Not before the elders,' she said.

'Please, aunt,'

'That's better.' She placed the tray on the table.

I was sure that she was happy. At least happier than before. Yassin tasted the harisah, licked his fingers, and said, 'God protect those hands.' She lowered her eyelids, embarrassed.

Occupied Palestine – Beer Al-Sab'a – 1985

He opened his eyes, but could not see anything. The cloud whited out whatever was there around him. Shit, he wouldn't be able to make out the two-legged giants. If they attacked him, how could he defend himself? He blinked and tightened his eye muscles. The place was full of them. His heart started beating like the jungle drums announcing danger. They walked towards him, then stared at him closely. Too close. Too near. Shit.

'Shadeed, my hero, my name is Husam. I am from Nablus too.'

All foggy but for one eye. One big eye full of water.

'I am Dirar, Khalid, Tawfiq, Rawhi.'

Sounds mixed together made no sense to him. Why didn't they leave him alone? They might fancy stepping on him. One of them touched his left leg. He stood on all six, stretched his feelers and hissed, 'Go away. Out.'

'Good God.' The giant placed his head between his bent legs. 'God help his mother.'

'Stay away from me.'

'We'll take good care of him. Every day, someone will give him his pills, wash and dress him.'

'Throw him out. I'm going nuts.'

'Khalid, he's quite harmless. Can't you see he's afraid of us?'

'Have mercy, throw him out!'

They left him alone. He was relieved. Out of danger. He squatted and emptied his bowels.

'I'm going nuts. My head will explode. Shitting around!'

'It's your turn, Khalid.'

The giant pushed him away and scrubbed the floor. Was he digging for grains? He crawled to his nest. Oh, where was she? He screamed, 'I want her. Where is she?' He went on screaming, then banged his head on the nest's wall. Let it collapse over his head. Fall down. His legs became lighter. The sun's belly danced in the distance. Now here. Now there. Now dark. Now light. 'Heh, heh.' He liked that game. He saw her walking on the soil. 'Hey, wait!' he shouted and ran after her. 'Why did you leave me?'

She smiled and said, 'I've promised never to leave you.'

'When I see you, this dancing sun goes through me and dances inside my chest. It tickles me and fills me with warmth.' He took her hand and said, 'Let's walk to the oasis.' When they stood near the pool, he asked her, 'Would you like to drink?' They dipped their heads in the water. The green fish swam around their heads, then got entangled with the sticky blue plants. 'Lovely, aren't they?'

'Yes,' she said. She adored him. He was lovely.

The water refreshed him. They walked back, but the green fish followed them. 'Why?'

'Maybe she's hungry.'

'I have some grains in my mouth. I'll give her some.' The fish was not interested. 'They don't speak, do they?'

'I know why she followed us, because she saw the glow coming out of your chest. You captured the sun inside.' 'Ha Ha Ha,' they laughed together. His voice became husky when he sang,

'You left without saying good-bye.
The tear glistened in my eyes.
This is my destiny.
Sun of my life set, set, sink.'

The giants surrounded him. Would they ever leave him alone? They suffocated him and made him feel like fighting again. The Rawdah neighbourhood attacked the camp. They stoned them. Wherever he looked he saw flying stones. Draw up a plan and attack suddenly. We need jungles, not plains. He wished that they wouldn't step on him. Terror is to terrorize. The still air of the cave made breathing impossible. Explosives, Molotov cocktails. He rubbed his face in a frenzy. Organized and systematic violence. Please have some food. Too close. Too near. Danger. Red. Sting.

'You must eat, my boy.'

If he came any closer, he would sting him. 'Go away. I'll sting you. It's poisonous.' He put the food container in front of him and walked away. His legs spread to the sky. He wished that they would not step on him. He put his joggling head into the bowl and sucked some grains.

'The best thing is to dilute them in water and give it to him.'

'And your Lord comes and the angels in ranks.'

'Throw him out please.'

He relieved himself. Amazing. His head grew lighter as if it wanted to fly. He stretched his legs and sighed. His head had wings. He missed her and wanted to give her some warmth from the sun captured in the chest. 'Mmm,' he murmured, and went to sleep.

'Today is my turn. I'll help you wash yourself.'

'Don't come any closer,' he hissed. They hated him and were jealous of him. They would step on him. 'Just because you don't have six legs like me.'

'I want to give you a bath.'

He shivered. Two big eyes stared at him and the rest of the face was eaten up by the cloud. He raised his leg and covered his face. The giant rubbed his back.

'I don't want to hurt you, my son. I'll never hurt you. Please let me help you wash your body.'

Big smiling eyes at the end of a blurred triangle. The monster didn't step on him. Why not? He crawled back to his nest. He carried him.

'It's all right, it's all right.'

He stopped shivering and looked around him. Yes, that was not bad. He liked that game. He giggled and said, 'Again.' He put him down under the running water and rubbed his body. It was like dipping his head in the pool, but where was the green fish? 'Heh, heh. Tickle my side legs.'

'Of course.' He put him down and covered him with rugs. It was hot.

'Let me go. The sun is imprisoned in my chest. Can't you see the glow?' Boiling hot. With his legs, he tore apart the heavy cover and crawled to his nest.

He saw her crawling towards him. Heh, heh. She came back. 'Welcome, welcome.' He raised his head and hissed, 'Where have you been? I missed you. I dreamt about you.'

'I just wandered about.'

'Ha, ha, ha. Do you want to eat?' He gave her the grains he had stored for winter.

'Why are you so happy?'

'She came back.' Always watery eyes. He knew they hated him.

'Who is "she"?'

'Are you blind? Can't you see her?' He pointed his feelers.

'That bloody ant. Throw him out. I can't take it any more.'

'"Have we not given him two eyes, and a tongue and two lips?"'

'Shut up, he's a hero.'

'Yes, he is.'

'Not like you, Dirar.'

'No, not like me.'

Why were they shouting at him? He went back to his nest and took her with him. 'Don't disappear again.'

'No.' Oh, how she loved him.

'Look at my chest. Can you see the glow? Move closer, I'll keep you warm. You want to go to sleep? Next to me? Mmm, I'll sing you something.'

'Yes please,' she said and moved closer to him. He hissed:

> 'Together, we were brought up,
> Together, we walked,
> Together, we spent our nights.
> Is it possible that parting will wipe out our
>   names?'

'Sad tune. I wish, Husam, that he'd improve, for his mother's sake.'

'Are you warm enough, darling?'

'Yes, love.'

'You know that I love you.'

'I love you too.'

'The wind takes us and brings us back
Until our families look for us.'

He placed his head on the floor and scratched his legs. The nest was dark. He couldn't see her properly.

While he was playing with her outside, one of them came closer to him. Those creatures wanted to hurt him.

'Shadeed, my boy, your mother will come to see you today.'

'I visited her yesterday,' he said and shrank in his nest.

'I won't hurt you, believe me.'

He couldn't be hurt any more. The giant touched his head lightly.

'Would you like to play with me?'

'Yes, yes.'

'Throw him to his mother, I'm going nuts.'

'Shut up, his finger-nail is more precious than you, informer!'

What were they saying? He stretched his feelers. No, better not to understand. What the eye doesn't see . . .

'I want him to look decent when his poor mother sees him.' He carried him to the waterfall and splashed him.

'I don't want to play,' he hissed.

'All right, my boy.' He took him back to his nest and tried to squeeze him into a piece of cloth.

'No, it's hot.'

'Please, Shadeed, stop fighting.'

He wrapped him in something and carried him outside. 'Stay in my lap.' The game had started. 'You are as light as my child.'

'Please let me see my son, Shadeed, before I go to my grave.'

'Hajjeh Amina, here, here.'

She came closer to the wire net and stared at his face. 'Where is Shadeed?'

'Here in my lap, mother.'

'That thing is not my son.'

'He is, I am sorry.'

He blinked and tightened his eye muscles. That creature was not a huge giant like them. He felt she was harmless and he liked her.

'Please, Hajjeh Amina, don't look so shocked. Talk to him.'

'Shadeed, Shadeed, my soul, don't you recognize me?'

He joggled his head and stretched his feelers.

'Shadeed, please answer me.'

That cover was too heavy on his back.

'Hajjeh Amina, keep your voice low.'

'Don't you remember your father, God bless his soul?'

He crept under the cover.

'It's all right.'

'God give me patience. Eman – don't you remember her? She passed the exam.' He gazed at her with his bulging eyes. Through the white cloud, he saw her hands pressed to the wire net. She placed them on her chest.

'Are you all right?'

'I'm fine, Dirar, it's just my chest. Sometimes it completely closes in . . . My love, my heart, speak to me. Maybe he is shy after all this time. Why are you wrapping him up like that?'

'He has a cold, so I thought this would keep him warm.'

'He stares as though he's blind.'

'No, no, he's just tired.'

Her eyes stared at him: he stirred under the cover.

She touched her neck with her hand. 'Is it true, what they say? Is it true that he has gone mad?'

'No, mother, they lied, don't worry. He is a little bit ill.'

'Almost bones, my soul. Do they feed him properly?'

'Yes, good food.'

'Dirar, God lengthen your life, please tell me the truth. I will accept God's will.'

'Believe me, he is exhausted and ill.'

'I am raising two chickens for him. When he is released, I'll slaughter them. I'll cook him musakhan, he likes that. Dirar, I want to see his wedding before I die.'

'You will. Try to talk to him.'

'Shadeed, Shadeed, talk to your mother. Talk to me please.'

He stretched his feelers and stood up on all six legs, then joggled his head. He was tired of that game and wanted to go back to his nest. The monster rubbed his head and hugged him. He lay quiet and closed his eyes. Couldn't they see the sun imprisoned in his chest, boiling, burning him? It was giving light. 'Heh, heh.'

'I beg you, talk to me, say something.' Tears ran from her eyes and her hands were pressed hard on the net wire. 'Say something to your mother.'

He wanted to crawl down. Enough. He tried to go down the giant's legs, but he pulled him upwards. He raised his abdomen, his hind feet, stretched his feelers and opened his jaws wide. 'Put me down,' he hissed.

'Please, stay here.'

'Leave me alone.'

'His voice has changed.'

'Possibly the cold.'

'God heal his wounds and take his hand.'

When he tried to crawl down, the giant pulled him

194

up again. 'I'll sting you. It's poisonous, you filthy monster,' he screamed and rubbed his feet together. The cover slipped down.

'Why is he naked? Why? Tell me.'

'He has a fever.'

'He's not walking.'

'Shadeed, come back to your mother.' The giant carried him and wrapped him again. 'Stay here, the game is not over yet.'

'Dirar, why did you lie to me? He *is* mad.' She pulled something white and jumped in the air.

'Heh heh.'

'Ya ya ya, he followed his father and brothers. Ya ya ya, why did you leave me alone? Ya ya ya, take me with you my beloved. Don't leave me here alone. Oh God, my heart.'

Familiar? He used to enjoy that game. He hissed, 'Ya Ya Ya.'

The giant placed him on the floor. 'The poor woman went mad too. She broke my heart.' The words for him were like vague shapes hanging in the air. They began infiltrating into his head. Sounds, mixed sounds. He couldn't find her. Where was she? He wanted her. He banged his head on the wall.

'It's all right.'

'Where in hell are his pills?'

One of the giants wiped the blood and gave him some water. He wanted her. Where was she? 'Mmm,' he moaned, then crawled towards the giant. He stared at him. His head hurt him. Pain. 'Mmm,' he hissed and rubbed his head on the giant's feet.

'It's the first time he has come near me willingly.

195

Come, come, my sweet boy.' The giant hugged him, and the warmth of touch calmed him down. Running his feet on a steep road. Searching for a gap in which his feet would fit. Somewhere to belong . . .

'I promised his mother I'd take good care of him.' He rocked him in his lap and lulled him to sleep, singing,

> 'Together we were brought up,
> Together we walked . . .'

He shuddered. His feet fitted in that gap. No more floating. He opened his jaws, sighed and went to sleep.

The Democratic State of Ishmael – Rahmah – 1984

One night, while I was studying in the kitchen, my mother rocked her chair and said, 'Eman, your uncle said "yes". You can go to Nablus with Sammah.'

I threw the book in the air and jumped to my feet. 'Did he?'

'Yes, love.'

'I wonder why he changed his mind?'

'I don't know.'

'Anyway, it's great.'

'Maybe he wants you to find a husband there.'

'A what?'

'I think that's what he had in mind when he agreed.'

That uncle of mine wanted to get rid of me.

'I'd better tell Sammah, because she said that it takes time to get a pass from here. The permission from the occupation authorities arrived last week.'

When I told Sammah, she kissed me. 'Wonderful, wonderful. I promise you an unforgettable trip.'

'It's my first.'

She laughed and said, 'You missed a lovely one with the Yank.'

'Yes, I missed the one with Tal'at.'

She waved her hankerchief in the air and started singing,

'Hey, girl, I am not English.

Why are you speaking with me in English?
I don't want you to say, "How are you?"
Or "I love you".'

'Do you need anything besides my passport?'
'Yes, two photos.'
'When do you think we'll get the permit?'
'Two weeks from now. Hopefully, we'll leave Rahmah on the second of April.' She began singing again.
'What's happening? You're in a good mood.'
'Of course. I'm getting married to Hani when we come back from the West Bank.'
I hugged her and said, 'Oh, I am happy for you.'
'I hope you'll find Mr. Right soon.'
My heart stirred. Was I capable of love? My father had taken a piece of my heart with him. And you need a complete heart in order to fall in love.
'Eman, I want you to get rid of those rags you keep wearing. Try to sew one or two decent dresses.'
'Sammah, these are not rags.'
'It's your mother's skirt. Isn't it?'
'Yes.'
'It's high time you took more care of your appearance. Hani told me that I turn him on when I'm dressed up.'
'Gosh, you went that far with him?'
'We even kissed,' she said and grinned like a naughty child.
'Sammah, take care.'
'Don't worry, nobody saw us.'
'What was it like?'
'Well, when he touched my lips I couldn't see the stars. Mind you, it was cloudy that night.'
We were giggling when Um-Arrtin came into the room. 'Eman, please help me with this.' She pointed at the half-stitched hem.

'Sure.'

Um-Arrtin smiled when I asked her permission. 'Of course, my daughter.'

'Will you manage alone until the middle of May?'

'Yes, don't worry. I'll ask Zakieh to take your place until you come back. Eman, if you pass the exam you won't come here any more, will you?'

'No, I'll try to find a job as a teacher.'

'So this will be a good test for Zakieh. I might hire her permanently.'

'She's a nice girl.'

'Very poor too.'

I was restless that night. What did Palestine look like? What happened to the Palestinians after the occupation? Would the Israelis harm me because I was an Arab? I felt excited and afraid. Malik crossed the floor on his tiny feet and stood near the bed. Then he sighed and lay down beside me. 'What's wrong, Malik?'

He rubbed his bright eyes and said, 'Eman, my sister, the boys at school asked me about my father. I didn't know what to say.'

I opened my arms and hugged him. 'Don't take any notice of them. They'll stop asking stupid questions soon.'

'Eman, why don't I have a father like other boys?'

Oh God. It was Malik's turn to be scalded, to get burned in the neighbourhood's flames. 'Our father is dead. He fought our enemy and the enemy killed him. You should be proud of him, becuse he's a hero.'

Malik nodded his head, but I was sure that he didn't understand. One day he would. I lulled him to sleep with a song:

> 'Go to sleep, Malik. Go to sleep.
> Hey, pigeons, don't be sad because
> Malik wants to go to sleep.'

Jud woke David up with her soft kisses. 'Wake up, lazybones. The sun rose a long time ago. The dew has evaporated and left the petals thirsty and waiting for the next dawn. The birds have reluctantly left their nests to bring food for their young ones. The bees, the butterflies – everything is humming, buzzing.'

'Jud, love, are you feeling all right?' David rubbed his eyes.

'I've never felt better.'

'You're smiling all over your face. Shoot.'

'I want to tell you something . . . something we've waited for all our lives.'

He tried to stop his hands from shaking. Was it possible after all these years? Stop building up your hopes, you fool. Maybe she wants to tell you that she's got a rise or she's been appointed headmistress of the kindergarten. Calm down.

She touched his face and said, 'Dav.' She couldn't complete the sentence. Her voice began shaking and her eyes were full of tears when she finally said, 'Dav, I'm pregnant.' Was he hallucinating again? He kissed her wet face to make sure that she was real. 'How did you know? I mean, when? I mean . . .'

'I waited three whole days. I'm sure. I got the results of the test this morning. It says, "Pregnancy

200

test – Mrs Dzentis – positive." Positive, David, positive.'

He jumped out of bed and said, 'Open the windows, open the doors. Let's have some sunshine in this house.' She was laughing and crying at the same time. 'Thank God. Thank God.' He knelt down, kissed her belly, stuck his head between her thighs and cried. He had brought a life into the world after all. 'So I *am* a man,' he said.

'And I'm a complete woman. I'll be a mother soon. I won't stare at other people's children any more, wishing one of them was mine. Do you know, sometimes when I touched their fluffy hair, pain ran from my hand up to my heart.'

'We'll have a clan of our own.' They laughed.

Over breakfast, David began to think about money. How much would raising a child cost? Would he be able to quit his job after all? He sipped his coffee and said, 'Jud, all the same, I'll leave that prison.'

'It would be nice if we gave our child a good life.'

'I also want to be a good father, and teach my child the morals of the Torah. I want to show him the difference between right and wrong and I should be in a position to do so.' When he spoke the words they sounded strange. Him? A father? He couldn't believe it. When the nurse slapped his baby's bottom and it cried, would he believe it then? In the meantime, he would make sure that Judith got the right treatment. 'You must see a doctor. He'll tell us what to do. Now, you need vitamins and rest.'

'You're an amateur.' They laughed.

'I'm going to hand in my resignation today. We'll start a new life together. A fresh one.' His body was lighter when he ran to the car. He felt young. No, he *was* young. He would live forever. If not him, his children would. He waved to Jud and drove off to the prison.

201

Occupied Palestine – Nablus – 1984

Sammah took her mother's hand and led her to one
of the benches under the iron umbrella. I sat next to
her. All the travellers who wanted to cross Damya
Bridge had to wait in that waiting-hell. The heat of
the valley made everybody nervous, especially the
policemen who were supposed to stamp our papers.
'Hey, donkey, don't you understand Arabic? Sit
down,' one of them shouted. The old man dragged
his feet along the whitish sand and sat on the ground
near our bench. His white kaftan and white head-
dress emphasized the darkness of his skin. His
expression was fixed. I took his bundle and said,
'Grandfather, why not sit next to us?'

'God bless you, my daughter. I like to be close to
the soil,' he said. He was counting the beads of his
green rosary. From the GTI group: God willing –
Tomorrow – It's all right.

Most of the women were wearing their national
dress. Old men too: but the younger generation
preferred the cool safari. I wondered how many
Palestinians lived outside their homeland.

'They separated us, God damn them,' Sammah's
mother said and wiped her wet forehead.

'Don't worry, mother. One day for you, another
against you. We shall return.'

'How?' I asked, and realized how theoretical and

202

dry my knowledge of the Palestinian issue was,

'The P.L.O. is giving the Zionists hell. I'm sure we'll go back one day.' Sammah never spoke like that. She never discussed those things with me. I saw another face of a friend I thought I knew well.

'Sammah, you know how I lost my father. How did you lose yours?'

'In the 1967 war. The Zionists killed him because he resisted the occupation.'

What a reason! Daddy resisted oppression too. If you resisted, you got killed.

'They wanted our land and "Welcome" on top of it.'

I remembered what my father once told his friends: 'Palestinians suffered a lot because of our weakness and disunity. We must return to Islam and the Qur'an to liberate the Iqsa Mosque. If you lose everything you once had, what can you do?' I looked at the miserable people around me who wanted to have a glimpse of their villages and almost saw the red flames scalding them.

Abu-Mustaffa, the old man sitting on the ground, started singing:

'Sabha is an old woman
Sixty years old.
Her heart is green, green, green.
Like an old tree –
As old as the earth.
Her son Mohammad will soon be nine
But he knows how to throw stones!
And he knows how to shout, "Oh, Palestine".'

Everybody repeated with him, 'Oh, Palestine. Oh, Palestine.'

'What a strong voice!'

'When we were in our country it was even stronger. Those were the days, my daughter. Those were the days,' he said, and wiped his tears.

'Where are you going?'

'To Nablus and then if the authorities give me a pass I'll cross to Rammla.'

'Do you have relatives there?'

He moved his body forwards and then backwards, scratched his head, fixed his head-dress and said, 'I lost three of my children in 1948 and in 1967 I lost thirteen of my children and grandchildren. My old lady too. Now, I live in a refugee camp away from our soil. An olive branch is dearer to me than my soul. The smell of the brown soil!'

'You will return, Abu-Mustaffa,' I said, sounding unconvincing even to myself.

'I don't want to be buried in one of the camps.'

'God forbid,' said Um-Sammah.

'Look,' said Sammah, pointing at a sparkling Polman bus, 'the tourists are allowed to go straight through. No inspection. We're searched like thieves on the way into our own country. Bloody tourists – they zoom past without even looking at us shabby natives.'

'Hey, take it easy.'

'It's unfair. The world is crazy,' she said in a trembling voice.

'God is up there,' Um-Sammah said.

A policeman read our names and said, 'Your turn.' We walked towards the bridge. The greenery of the river banks was amazing. What a lovely, serene place! When I saw the Israeli flag fluttering, the scene became colourless, as if the colours had washed away in a wink. A white cloth with two blue strips and David's star in the middle. Sammah whispered, 'The blue strips are the Nile and the Euphrates. They want their Biblical kingdom back.'

'What? More land?'

The wood of the bridge creaked under our tired feet. When we reached the end of the bridge, I saw four Israeli soldiers pointing their machine-guns at us. I shivered and looked at Sammah. Her eyes were full of anger. We queued to be inspected. I entered a small room. A muscular policewoman said to me, 'This way.' I looked around me open-mouthed. Beeping walkie-talkies, screens, computers. All this high technology, and Al-Rabia' neighbourhood was still without telephones! It was another world, and I did not understand it because the keys to it were not in my hands.

'Take off your clothes.'

I was surprised. Sammah should have explained the procedure to me. I fumbled with the buttons of my shirt, hoping that the big woman would change her mind. 'Come on. Your underwear too.' I stood naked and shivering between them. It was the first time I had taken off my clothes in front of a stranger. She ran a device over them and threw them on the floor. 'You are not allowed to take cosmetics with you,' she said and took away my eyeshadow and lipstick, the only luxury items I had. Hanin had given them to me as a present. I left the spaceship and walked outside. The sun was hidden behind the trees. A group of soldiers in their khaki uniforms and sunglasses sat under a huge tree, drinking Coke from cans. Holiday-makers – they were like the American tourists who roamed the streets of Rahmah. I couldn't believe that they were soldiers of the Israeli force that had beaten the Arab armies twice. The holiday-makers had decided to settle in the virgin country and were trying to forget about the primitive natives.

Abu-Mustaffa collected his things and tied up his bundle again. Some Palestinians were delayed and we had to move on without them. The bus driver put his handkerchief around his collar, said 'In the name of God' and started the engine. The passengers were silent, as if the Israelis had confiscated their tongues too. Abu-Mustaffa placed his hand on his cheek and sighed. Sammah clasped her hands and her mother looked at the sky. The driver said in a calm but clear voice, 'It's all right. God will dispel our sorrow.'

We went up the winding road towards Nablus. I felt relieved to be out of the whitish heat of the valley. Palestine was more fertile than Rahmah. The occupation was everywhere – barricades, patrol cars, tanks, soldiers. It was like a military base. Sammah gritted her teeth when she saw the soildiers. 'If I don't say something, I'll explode.' She started reciting Mahmoud Darwish's poetry:

> 'My homeland! O Eagle that sheaths its beak of
> flame
> In my eyes
> Through the wooden bars.
> All that I possess in the presence of death
> Is a forehead and an anger.'

'Please, Sammah, calm down. Look at that flock of birds – over there.'

They landed, decorating the citrus trees with their wings.

'Eman, I've never smelled a more pleasant scent.'

The smell made me feel that all the pain I had been through was a joke. I was healed. The sun gave me warmth and made me feel full. My body became so light and trasparent that the birds flew through me. Oh, Palestine. Some old houses appeared on the horizon. 'That's Nablus,' said Sammah. A big town sleeping at the feet of Al-Nar mountain. We went round the roundabout. The distinct character of the city struck me. Stone houses with verandahs and fountains, some of them going back to the 19th century when the Mamlukes were the rulers of the Arab world. The city centre was not modernized in any way. The small shops had wooden doors instead of the stainless steel that had invaded Rahmah. Nablus was a jump into the past with all its miseries and glory.

'This city is the symbol of steadfastness,' whispered Sammah.

I looked at the faces of the people and realized that something was missing. Smiles. No smiling faces. Another Al-Rabia' neighbourhood? We went down the steps of the bus and an Israeli soldier checked our papers. How many times were they going to do that? Um-Sammah fumbled in her handbag looking for her paper. The soldier shouted, 'Move!' in his funny Arabic. The papers were not in her bag. He pushed her and she fell down.

'What do you think you're doing? Can't you see she's an old woman?' Somebody pulled my arm, then pushed me behind the bus. I was going to tell the soldier what I thought of him, but somebody whom I couldn't see had shut my mouth with his hand. As I struggled to get free, I heard him whispering, 'I am a Palestinian. You must not abuse the Israelis. Are you mad? They'll take you and then the blue flies won't be able to find you.' The strong hands released me. I looked at him. He was a dark young man. He smiled and said, 'I'm sorry.' I stared at him silently. He gave me his right hand and introduced himself: 'Shadeed Mahmud Al-Falastini.' I shook his hand and said in a hoarse voice, 'Eman Saqi.' When he went back to help Um-Sammah the sun caught his curly brown hair.

Um-Sammah found her papers under the seat and the soldier let her pass. Shadeed took her hand and said, 'Lean on me, mother.'

'God bless you, my son.'

'Your daughter has a hot temper.'

'She's my daughter's friend.'

He introduced himself to Um-Sammah and Sammah and said, 'It's better if you take a taxi.'

We took a taxi to the camp. A distinctive stink struck me, but by the time we arrived at the camp's centre I had got used to it. The camp was similar to our neighbourhood. More trees were planted between the shacks than we had in the so-called 'spring' neighbourhood.

'Welcome, welcome,' Sammah's aunt said, 'Time has brought us together again.'

Um-Ahmad served the tea and I sipped it quietly. I felt restless and full of energy.

'What's wrong with you?' Sammah asked, 'You're so quiet.'

The shack was merely two big rooms and a small kitchen. Um-Ahmad had tried hard to make the sitting room bright. White sheets everywhere, over the pile of mattresses, on top of chairs. It must be hard work keeping them that white.

'Eman, why don't you go with Sammah for a walk? Have a look at the camp and the surrounding area.'

'All right.'

The sun was setting behind the shacks and the alleys of the camp glowed with light and children's laughter. I saw the shining brown hair. Where was he?

'Good afternoon,' he said and I almost jumped. 'How are you?'

Warm fluid coursed through me and my face felt blazing hot. His quizzical expression made me even more hot and embarrassed.

'You are guests here?'

'Yes, we came from Rahmah to visit my uncle, Abu-Ahmad.'

'Of course.'

'How long are you going to stay here?'

Another flush of heat.

'About two months.'

'See you later,' he said and walked away.

Sammah eyed me and said, 'What's going on, Miss Eman?'

I shrugged. I wished I knew what was happening to me.

Right next to the camp a big house sat as if it were a big dog guarding the scattered shacks. 'It's marvellous,' I said.

'It belongs to the Hasibs – they're one of the rich families of the area.'

A high wall encircled the two-storey house and the citrus and olive trees leaned their branches on the walls. I could hear the sound of water trickling.

'A fountain?'

'Yes. Unfortunately the owner has gone to live in one of the Arab countries. There's an old madman from the camp guarding the place.'

I closed my eyes and imagined the lady coming down the stairs or taking coffee with her friends on the verandah. I wanted to go inside and catch a glimpse of the past, which I could smell.

'It's almost six o'clock. We should be getting back. The curfew will start soon.'

'What curfew?'

'A security curfew from six to six. Nobody is allowed to leave the camp.'

'What if you have an emergency?'

'You need special permission from the Military Governor.'

When we entered the house, Um-Ahmad said, 'Abu-Ahmad didn't come back. God protect him.'

'Where does he work?'

'In 48 Palestine.'

'You mean with the Jews?'

'No, Eman, *for* the Jews.'

'Why?'

'Because if he didn't travel all that distance every day we would die of hunger.'

The Arabs worked for the Jews? 'Why not have their own shops?'

They looked at me and shook their heads.

When we were nearly asleep, I said to Sammah, 'He's so attractive.'

'Who?'

Shadeed.'

'Mmm.'

The sun boiled in his head. He could hear the bubbling. The blaze of that belly dancer melted him. When the longing touched his heart it melted. Evaporated. His face was wet and some drops of water clung to the hair on his legs. How could he get rid of that planet? Too close to the fire. He crept out of his nest into the desert. Where were the palm trees hiding? Thin black pillars and a glare of orange behind. The pool should be there. He dug his legs deep into the soil in order the reach the cold layer. The sound of the bubbling increased. He dipped his head in the water. As if touched by a witch it began boiling immediately. The steam filled the oasis and the shadows of palm trees became taller. Apparitions in the dark. He shuddered and crawled back to his nest. Those trees would collapse on him and flatten his body against the soil. 'Leave me alone. Just a small insect.' The trees followed his light. Burning-penetrating-exploding beams. A formidable example of what can be achieved with discipline, organization and revolutionary spirit.

When he looked around him he could make out two foggy eyes. He blinked and they moved away from him. He might step on him, kill him or press his body to the ground. He lay down and the dampness reached his skin. The bubbling calmed down. He wished that the sun would leave his skull.

'He has a fever.'

'I hope he dies soon.'

'"And those who disbelieve in Our communications, they are the people of the left hand."'

'Shut up.'

'Give me the pill.'

The voices intermingled like the blue plants in his head. They annoyed him with those sounds. They tried to attract his attention. He would never look at them. No mercy. He joggled his head and said, 'We decided that you will all rot in Hell.'

'Khalid, repeat after me: A, B, C, D, E.'

He stretched his feelers to listen to the familiar sounds. A-B-C, 1-2-3. One of them drew a line on the floor. 'Can you read this? Khalid can you? Tawfiq?' He tightened his eye muscles, joggled his head and crawled a little bit closer. 'I gave you those letters yesterday. Try to read it.' He moved closer to the circle. He could only make out some backs and heads. He wanted to learn something new in order to impress her when she came. He crept on until he was right behind them.

'Can you read this, Shadeed?'

He blinked and hissed, 'Mmm . . . er . . . f-ather.'

'Wonderful.'

'The wonder-kid.'

'What a bright boy!'

He joggled his head. The words made sense to him. A gentle hand massaged all the tissues of his body. Warm feeling. They were always crying, those giants.

'I swear to God, Dirar, he's improving. . . . Shadeed, do you know what this word means?'

'Mmm, but there are two kinds of fathers. Real and frauds.'

212

'Yes, of course.'

'The wonder-kid.'

'Clap your hands for Shadeed.'

They applauded, and he felt so embarrassed that he galloped to his nest. When the rushing heat stopped he crawled back and asked, 'I want to draw.'

'Of course.'

He handed him the chalk but he couldn't grab it.

'I'll teach you how to carry things.'

'I'll do it with my teeth.'

'Use your legs.'

He took his front leg and bent his joints.

'See, you can hold it.'

He crawled around the room six times, as quickly as he could. He roared with laughter, then joggled his head. 'Again,' he hissed.

He wanted to scribble on the floor like them. When they were all asleep he chalked a line on the floor. He gritted his teeth and drew another line. Heh, heh. He imitated the giants. He wanted to fill the world with lines. He wiped it away with his feet and it disappeared. White dust stuck to the hair at the end of his legs. The ·flour was diffused through the tent. When they woke up he would surprise them.

'Give me a chalk.'

'Give him whatever he asks for.'

They rubbed their faces and stared at him. He could see them through the hazy cloud. He drew two squares, then framed them with a circle. Some flowers were sticking out of the squares.

'Explain, Shadeed.'

'It's called the martyrs. These flowers are their blood.'

They shouted at him and jumped. 'Great, great.' They were getting jealous of him, he knew it. His

213

joints trembled with fear. They might kill him or step on him and crush his abdomen. 'No, please,' he hissed and crawled back to his nest. He counted 1, 2, 3. He waited for the avalanche. His nest would collapse soon. His face and legs were wet. Why did they want to kill him? He curled into himself. Would the bundle survive the fluid? The sun began boiling again. Bubble. Bubble. The heat in his skull scalded him. 'Thirsty.' The pain. It hurt and stung. 'Thirsty.'

'Drink, my boy.'

The water ran down his throat, but nothing would put out that blazing fire. He banged his head. Bang, bubble, bang. 'Thirsty,' he shouted and fell down to the ground.

'They said that I am a bright boy, my darling.'

'Well, you are.'

'I drew a picture, but they became jealous of me. They wanted to kill me.'

'Don't show them your skill. They'll envy you,' she said and pulled a grain from his nest. 'Let's go for a walk.'

'No, I'm afraid of the sun. Bubble, bubble, bang.'

'My poor baby, I'll push it out of you.'

'Thank you, darling.'

They walked on the yellow sands and avoided looking at the sky above. Maybe it would sink into his head. He would command her to go. He looked at her and noticed how attractive she was. He wanted to do something with her.

'Let's take a break. I can't move my legs.'

'Fine, darling.'

He lay down and rubbed his legs together. To touch her. Touch her. He said to her, 'Come here.'

'No, I'm shy of you.'

'Move closer.' He climbed onto her back and said, 'It's lovely when you're close to me.' She moved her

214

body underneath him and a strange feeling overtook him. Magic. He slid on her upwards, then downwards. Still, he felt that he was not close enough. Upwards, downwards. Flash. A quiver annihilated him from the desert. His pain and life vanished in a wink. A drop of water absorbed by the blazing sands. Even the bubbling sun evaporated. Trembling with joy, he released her and roared with laughter, 'Ha Ha Ha Ha.'

'You look so happy today.'

'Mmm, yes.' Never tell him your secret. He giggled.

'I want you to help me.'

'Help you?'

'Yes, you are bright and you know how to draw.'

He joggled his head.

'Could you draw these letters again?'

'Mmm, I'll try.'

His heart was beating fiercely when he held the chalk. His ribs burst with pride. Shit, he couldn't see.

'Take your time.'

'Husam, I know that he'll do it, but please all of you react calmly to his success.'

'We don't want to frighten him off.'

'Samood gave the lie in their inordinacy.'

He drew the curve of B. He lay flat on his belly and the cool floor made him feel so relaxed. When he finished the C he felt exhausted so he crawled towards the giant and rubbed his head with his legs. The giant swung him in the air, then put him in his lap. First, he became like a dry stick from fear, then he realized that the giant was playing with him so he giggled.

'Are you tired, my boy?'

'Mmm.'

'You did a wonderful job.'

'Except the seeking of the pleasure of his Lord, The Most High.'

215

'Good boy.'

He crawled closer to the giant and put his head on his chest. 'Dirar,' he hissed, 'I'm tired.' Dirar hugged him and started crying.

'Forgive me, Shadeed. Forgive me, my hero. I confessed,' he said.

'Good morning,' Shadeed said to me.

'Good morning.'

'Will you come for a walk? I got Abu-Ahmad's permission.'

'What?'

'Don't you want to come with me?'

A rush of faces. Malik, Bakir, Omar, my mother and Um-Musaad. Hanin had warned me several times of men. They want us hard to get, she said. Gosh, if my uncle saw me he would do what he wanted to do ages ago, he would kill me. My hands started shaking. 'I don't know,' I said, looking at the faces.

'We won't be long.'

I walked next to him hesitantly, taking care that there was enough distance between us. When we left the camp and were strolling near the big house, he asked, 'Is this your first visit to Palestine?'

'No, I came before the 67 War,' I said, looking at my toes.

'May I call you Eman?'

'Yes, if you like.'

We started walking uphill. He pointed at a flower and said, 'This flower is the red anemone.' He explained slowly, as if he was talking to a child.

'I am eighteen, you know.'

217

'Really? I wouldn't have given you more than twelve.'

'What?'

'You look like a deserted child.'

I was furious. 'You!' Why couldn't he see that I was a mature woman?

He grabbed my wrists and said, 'Violence is the last resort.' I dropped my hands and asked, 'Is this Al-Nar mountain?' I just wanted to change the discussion before my embarrassment got any worse.

'Yes, the revolutionary haven. All the fighters hide in its caves. I'll show you one of them.'

I chose a footpath and followed it slowly. He accepted my choice and went up behind me. He knew that area much better than I did, but all the same he didn't comment on my choice. I liked that very much: it gave me strength and self-respect.

He looked at the valley and said, as if talking to himself, 'My father died here in 1967 . . .'

'I am sorry,' I interrupted.

'Don't be. He's one of thousands who irrigated this land with their blood. His friend, Sheikh Masaud, told me that they found him hiding in one of the caves. He used to say, "The Bristish attacked us, then the Zionists. The same chase, but different faces".'

My father's hands were thin and rough. He used to run them over my hair and say, 'Eman, Mamma'. 'Yes, the same chase, but different faces.'

The sun shone from the middle of the sky. The red drops of the anemones gave a darker shade to the colour of the green grass and herbs.

'Our meadows and mountains are covered with this flower. It's the blood of the martyrs – that's what my mother said.'

My father's blood was trickling from the gallows to the cement yard. No chance of any flowers there.

'You look so sad, Eman.'

'So these are drops of blood from the martyrs?'

'Yes.'

I must stop standing in the dusty stations of the past and move to the present. What was done, was done. Nablus snuggled up to the mountain and was warm and comfortable. 'I can't believe that this land is occupied.'

'It's only your first time here after the war. They killed my father and nine brothers and sisters. I was young then. When I grew older and was able to understand the size of the calamity, you can't imagine the pain that struck me,' he said and sat down on the grass.

The pain he felt. I couldn't imagine the pain he felt. I sat down next to him. The ghosts of the past would always live in my mind, shaking my head with their laughter.

He was gazing at me and said suddenly, 'I like those dark eyes. They're black but they show every emotion.'

Something inside me swelled and blossomed. The same feeling I had when Tal'at tried to flatter me. This time, it was more fulfilling and quenching. Sweet words. The buzz of bees and the rustle of grass filled my ears. I was stroking a flower when I saw a worm moving. It was honey-coloured and shining. 'Earthworms, Shadeed. It's springtime,' I cried excitedly.

He took my hand and ran his fingers over my palm. Invisible strings in my limbs were drawn tight. I pulled my hand away. 'Let's go to the cave.' We stood up and started climbing. I went in front, and Shadeed gave me directions to the cave. 'Eman, turn left.'

I picked a leaf and asked what it was. The smell was familiar.

'Thyme. Don't you like it?'

'Are you kidding, it's our daily diet!' I rubbed the soft leaf and stuck it in my pocket. The smell of toast and tea mingled with the voices of my brothers, fighting over who was going to the toilet first, filled the air. I wondered what they were doing.

A sharp rock stood in front of us. 'The cave is right behind this rock.' He pushed the rock and I saw the entrance. It was well concealed. He took my hand, and we went in. I shivered because the place was cold and damp. The sunlight that penetrated through the narrow passage didn't reach far.

'This is one of the best hiding-places,' he said thoughtfully, then squeezed my hand. When he kissed my palm I realized that I had never been this close to a man before, except my father. The sound of Hanin's crying in the night rushed into my ears. He cupped my face in his dark hands. 'I wonder what caused that sadness.' When he pulled me towards him the warmth of his body seeped through my T-shirt. 'Fragile, thin, sad,' he murmured and kissed me. A closeness that heals all wounds but opens doors of raging desires for more closeness. My body erupted with goose pimples. Gosh, I shouldn't have done that. I disentangled myself and ran out of the cold cave. The bright light blinded me for a second, then I saw the town snuggled up against the mountainside. The buzz of bees shattered the silence. I resisted the need to go back and bury myself in his chest for good. My belly throbbed with strange pain – as if while running out of the cave, part of my body had fallen down to the ground.

He stood right behind me and without looking at him I said, 'You shouldn't – I mean we shouldn't have done that.'

'Why?'

'It's taboo.'

'Do you really believe in that rubbish?'

Using Hanin's words, I said, 'You men have a fixation on virginity. You like us to be hard to get. I swear that this was the first time I have ever been touched by a man.'

'I have a fixation on virginity? You don't know what you're talking about. Besides, you don't have to swear. It's obvious.' I blushed. He continued: 'What *is* the meaning of taboo?'

'Something that we shouldn't do,'

'Why?'

'Because it's forbidden.'

'Who says so?'

'People.'

'You mean old books, senile old women and stinking dervishes.'

'Gosh, you shouldn't say that.'

'Although I want you to discover your own truth by yourself, I will tell you just one thing. Nobody, absolutely nobody has the right to enforce a code of morals on you. You're an individual, a miracle. Always remember that.'

The only similar speech I had ever heard came from Shamma'eh. He was talking about something I couldn't fully understand. I couldn't absorb it, but all the same I respected it. I opened my mouth then closed it.

'And now, sad eyes, it's time to take you back home.'

Shadeed was unlike any man I had met before. He was different from my uncle because he treated me with consideration, and took whatever I said seriously. He was different from Tal'at who despised his country because Shadeed adored his. While we were walking one morning, he said, 'Palestine runs in my blood. Even if they expel me, we'll never part because it lives here,' he hit his chest. 'It's like a fungus on my skin.'

'Rahmah for me is the best place in the world. So-called "Mercy" – but mercy doesn't exist there. What hurts me most is the poverty. Shamma'eh, the garbage collector, has spent most of his life saving money to get married. When I left Rahmah, he was still a bachelor.'

'How old is he?'

'He must be in his forties. Why isn't everybody rich and happy?'

'Wherever a tyrant exists you'll find oppressed people. One day the'll get fed up and history will be put right.' I was beginning to know him, but I had never seen him so moved. He went on: 'When I was a schoolboy, I realized that we had no bread except what UNRWA handed to us. I asked myself, 'Why?' The Zionists occupied our country and reduced us to scattered beggars in the Arab world. When I saw my mother carrying a sack of flour and covered with white from head to toe – even her eyelashes were white – I decided to leave school. Education is a luxury for a refugee like me. Gibran had said, "Give me bread and I'll give you art." Don't give me bread and I'll give you destruction.'

'It's a luxury for people like me, too. I left school because I had to help my mother. I'll be a teacher one day.'

'What about your father?'

'Shadeed, they murdered my father.'

'Who did?'

'The tyrants.'

'What are you talking about?'

'My father tried to overthrow the government and

was trying to develop Islamic socialism. That's what people told me later. They arrested him, they gave him a show trial, and they hanged him in 1977.'

I felt so exhausted that I wanted to sit down. He took my hand and we sat down together on the ground. The sun trudged back to her world. I shivered.

'I'm sorry, Eman. I had no idea.'

I controlled my tears and said, 'No, no. I'm all right now. I'm quite all right. It's just my brothers and my mother. I am fine – really.' He hugged me. 'Shadeed, they killed Lulu.'

'Who's Lulu?'

'My doll,' I said and began crying as if the soldiers had stabbed Lulu at that moment and not fifteen years ago.

'It's all right. Don't cry,' he said and stroked my hair. With his warm tongue he licked the salty tears trickling down my face, and wiped away the black spot that had weighed upon my heart all that time. I don't know how long I cried on Shadeed's shoulder. When at last he said, 'Fine, stop crying, I'll buy you another doll,' I burst out laughing and my face was still wet. 'I know where I can get you one as a matter of fact. Al-Najjah University Bazaar will start tomorrow. Would you like to come with me?'

I stretched myself on the cold grass and said, 'I'll think about it.'

'Please,' he whispered in my ear, then kissed my neck. A tremor ran madly through my body and I wanted badly to pull him closer to me, but I saw a warning flash of red light so I pushed him away and said, 'Yes.'

'Sad eyes, I promise you that tomorrow will be better than yesterday and today.' In his brown eyes I saw a strange faith in the future: he trusted the future and I believed him, and believed in him.

'Eman, I hate using clichés but I think I love you.'

223

I ran my fingers through his hair. Something inside me was eager to be set free, a pressure that his words and touches were building up.

'Do you feel anything for me?'

Stay silent. What could I tell him? That everything I touched got burnt to ashes. That I sprinkled misery around me.

'Don't you like me?'

No. No.

'Answer me, Eman.'

'No!' I ran down to the camp and he came after me. I heard him talking to Sammah in the sitting room, then he pushed the door open and said, 'I want you to come with me.' I nodded and he closed the door.

Minutes later, Sammah rushed in saying, 'Are you crazy? He's one of the best men in the camp. He loves you. What more do you want?'

'I don't want to love or be loved by anyone.'

'Sorry, I can't understand you.'

How could she understand me when I couldn't understand myself? My need for Shadeed was so strong that it almost hurt. Never let go. The flames attacked my body from every direction. Rida, my father, Amal, Lulu and all the people in my neighbourhood. Hot tears ran wildly for the second time that day, and that made me shake with anger because it meant that I had broken my own rules. No tears. You stupid fool, no tears. I sobbed and cried that night over Rida who disappeared from my life suddenly, over Amal whom Um-Musaad slapped to death, over my father who died reciting the Qur'an, over my mother the grey bundle of bones, over Malik, over Hanin who spent days crying, even over Shamma'eh. I cried over every child that had been born and every pebble in the streets.

'Good morning, Um-Ahmad.' When I heard Shadeed's voice my hands began shaking. His presence was enough to turn my world upside-down. Instead of the usual khaki trousers, he was wearing that morning a grey pair and a light blue shirt. There was something about him that suggested he kept more to himself than he expressed. He was tougher than the boys of Al-Nahar neighbourhood, where my uncle's palace was, who put 'Mummy' between every two words. I straightened my skirt and touched my hair.

'You look lovely.' Sweet, sweet words.

'Are you enjoying your stay here?' he asked Um-Sammah.

'Yes, my son. It's enough for me to sit on my country's soil.'

'Will you excuse us,' he said to Um-Ahmad, who was breast-feeding her eighth child.

'God be with you.'

He kept the door open for me. When my elbow brushed his, my mind ran all over the place.

As we crossed the street, I noticed that all the shops were open.

'The strike came to an end yesterday. They forced the owners to open their shops.'

'Why were they on strike?'

'Because of the long curfew.'

'It's like living in a big prison,' said Sammah; and after that we stopped talking for some time. The presence of an occupier was becoming more tangible every passing day.

'You can't leave Nablus without eating konaffeh.' The pedlar was cooking it on the pavement. With his fingers he spread the paste in a big tray, topped it with cheese, then added syrup. Three minutes later the paste became glowing red and the cheese melted. He cut me a piece.

'Long live Sheikh Masaud,' said Shadeed. The pedlar whispered something in Shadeed's ear. 'Excuse me,' he said and moved a few steps with Sheikh Masaud. They were discussing something heatedly. Judging from Shadeed's expression, he was giving orders of some kind. I had never seen him look so serious before. There must be something about Shadeed that I didn't know.

They came back and smiled at us. Sheikh Masaud wiped his hands with his long apron, fixed his white cap and said, 'Take good care of this tough man.' I blushed and moved behind Shadeed. The pedlar could see that something was going on between us!

'You made her blush.'

We continued walking while eating. I licked the syrup and said, 'It's delicious.'

He stared at my lips and said, 'Sure is.'

In the distance, the university looked like a secondary school. 'Is that the university?'

'Yes, it's a humble one,' said Sammah.

'If you want to plant a tree in your garden you must get special permission from the Military Governor. He takes his time, and the result is humble buildings and services. Even a window-shield needs permission. The Arab areas become so disorganised.'

'If you want to build a wall, for example, do you need permission?'

'Anything. Also, we don't have enough money because nobody knows where we belong – administratively, that is.'

'Thank God, we have a university. The real problem, Eman, is not the building, it's the occupation. They close this university for no reason at all,' said Sammah.

'Simply speaking, they don't want us to stay here,

so they try to make life as hard as possible for Palestinians.'

'The students go to houses, mosques and schools to take their lectures when they shut down the university.'

'That's marvellous. So they continue their studying even if they have no proper place to do it. I want to be a teacher on day, Sammah, so I read a book once about teaching. The lecturers get rid of the artificial situation if they teach outside campus. It has its positive side,' I said.

The campus was encircled by hundreds of helmeted soldiers carrying shields and cudgels. Tanks, jeeps. 'Why?' I asked.

'Stay calm and walk slowly through the gate,' he said.

The soldiers were chatting in Hebrew. It sounded like Arabic because it has almost the same letters. Shadeed listened carefully.

'What are they saying?'

'This way, Sammah,' he said, ignoring my question.

Two armed soldiers checked our papers at the entrance and then one of them said, 'Come in' in Arabic and laughed. I saw a shining machine-gun dangled across his shoulder and I remembered the bayonets of the soldiers who attacked our house and killed Lulu.

We crossed a spacious yard covered with tarmac to a high building. 'Al-Najjah University Annual Charity Bazaar' was written in red on a big piece of cloth tied to the wall over the main entrance. The bazaar was held in a big hall where the students lined up tables and displayed on them the things they wanted to sell. We squeezed ourselves through until we reached the tables which were covered with flowers and embroidery. Shadeed greeted one of the sales girls and asked her for a national dress. She took one out from a box under the table. A black satin fabric embroidered with mauve threads. Eighteen dinars, she said.

'Do you like it?'

The way the mauve and violet threads were mixed fascinated me. 'Yes.'

He bought it and gave it to me. 'It's a souvenir.'

'Oh, no. It's too much.'

'Please, I want you to have it.'

'Thank you, Shadeed.' I was so touched by his present because I hadn't had one for a long, long time. The last gift I had was the velvet ribbon my father gave me in the festival. I lowered my head in order not to show him my glistening eyes.

We moved to another table. Camels were sculptured out of olive wood, jewellery boxes made of mother-of-pearl. The crowd pushed him closer to me. He whispered in my ear, 'Eman, love . . .' An explosion rocked the hall and some of the panes burst into the building. A cloud of smoke. I gasped for air and my tears ran down my cheeks. Shadeed put his hand around my waist, pulled Sammah's hand and pushed us through a side door. 'Go back to the camp, quickly. RUN!' He disappeared behind the cloud of smoke.

We ran and ran until we saw Sheikh Masaud. He waved to us and said, 'This way.' He led us through a narrow passage between the old houses. Suddenly we found ourselves in the camp.

'God help us, what happened?' asked Um-Ahmad when she saw our appearance.

'They broke into the university,' answered Sheikh Masaud.

'God punish them.'

228

'One of the kids raised the Palestinian flag.'

'Who did it?'

'Whoever it was, he's a hero. It's not a joke – he could get life.'

'God, can you see the misery, the humiliation?' said Um-Sammah, raising her hands towards the sky.

Where was Shadeed? If they took him, I would never see him again. Shadeed, Shadeed.

Hours later, he came back. his shirt was stained with blood and mud. 'Are you all right, my son?' asked Um-Ahmad.

'Yes, I am fine.' His face was as yellow as a lemon so I didn't believe him.

'Shadeed?' I asked.

'I'm fine, really.'

'I'd better go,' said Sheikh Masaud.

'Stay in the streets. The curfew will start soon.'

Um-Ahmad was breast-feeding her baby. Um-Sammah was invoking God, Sammah was sitting with her head in her hands and I was standing in the corner.

'Eman, I would like you to come with me to our house.'

'Now?'

'Yes, now. Excuse us,' he said and took my hand, then squeezed it. Shadeed was shivering? I asked the same question for the second time: 'Are you all right?'

'Yes. No. Shit. They took eighty-five students to jail. The stupid kids raised the flag. We told them not to do it!'

'We?'

He took both hands and pressed them to his chest. I felt that he wanted me to help him, support him, even save him. 'I don't know when this nightmare will end,' he said to himself.

When we went into the small hut at the other end of the camp, his mother welcomed us and asked, 'What happened, my son?'

'Nothing unusual. Mother, this is Eman.'

'He talked about you,' she said, staring at me. Hajjeh Amina was a small woman with a round face that was framed with a white veil. She pulled the end of her embroidered black dress and said, 'You should have told me. I would have prepared dinner for our guest.'

'Thank you, my mother,' I said. She went to the kitchen and he sat down on one of the chairs, then rubbed his eyes.

'Is it always like this?'

'Yes, I don't know when it will ever stop.'

I looked at the map of Palestine, which was framed in black, and his father's picture, and asked, 'Is there an end to it all?'

'I don't think so. Not in my lifetime, at least.'

I sat down on the floor leaning on his legs and said, 'I hate wars and fighting.'

'I hate wars too. But how can you bring about a radical political change without war?'

My heart leaped in my chest like an imprisoned sparrow. Shadeed was a Fedayee. I was sure. I inhaled some air and asked, 'Are *you* a Fedayee?' He didn't answer. 'Are you?' He remained silent. I said as calmly as possible, 'It's my destiny. The story of my life.'

It was the second time that day I had been left gasping for air. The first time was when they used tear-gas bombs, and the second was when I realized that he must be a guerilla fighter. I broke into a fit of weeping, holding his legs. My tears ran wildly down my cheeks, those bloody tears again.

He pulled me to my feet and asked, 'Why are you crying?'

'Oh, Shadeed.' I hugged him.

230

He kissed my wet lashes. 'Those beautiful eyes must not cry.'

We were interrupted by his mother. 'Dinner is ready.' He went to the kitchen and brought a big tray full of onion, chicken and rice. His mother brought a loaf and salad. The food was fresh and tasty. 'In the name of God,' Hajjeh Amina said and started eating.

'Thank you, my mother.'

She looked at me and said, 'Shadeed, this girl is so thin. Ask her to eat more.'

'Please, eat some more for my mother's sake.'

He was so hungry that he kept taking pieces of chicken and coming back for more. I couldn't think why he reminded me of Malik having his breakfast. His mother put down her piece of bread and said, 'I wonder where they are, my beloved ones?'

'My brothers and sisters,' Shadeed explained.

'They left me on my own.' Her dreamy eyes looked at the picture on the wall and added, 'I wish I'd buried him in the right position.'

There was a knock on the door and a handsome man rushed into the room. 'They took . . . '

'Adnan,' Shadeed said in a way that meant 'Stop talking.' It was an order.

'I must talk to you, now,' and he waved his hand to us.

'Wait for me outside.'

Although I couldn't understand what they were talking about because I couldn't hear them properly, I could see that there was an urgency in the discussion.

'My daughter, he talks a lot about you. He's my only son. I have nobody else in this world.' She tried to tell me something, but I couldn't understand what she was hinting at.

'Sorry,' he said and sat down next to me and continued eating. When we had finished, I did the washing-up and he put the plates back in the cupboard. I had a glimpse of about twenty empty Cola bottles.

'Collecting empty bottles must be one of your hobbies!'

He ignored my remark and said, 'You know, Mother likes you because she spoke about my brothers.'

I was so pleased to hear that Hajjeh Amina approved of me. He stood right behind me and said, 'You're not thin at all.' He moved closer and kissed the back of my neck. 'Eman, will you marry me?'

'Are you serious?'

'I want you to sleep next to me every day of my life. I want to see this face every sunrise.'

'I'm afraid that I'll lose you too.'

'No, you won't. Trust me.'

'I lost all the people I loved.'

'It has nothing to do with our marriage.'

'I don't know.'

'I promise I'll make you happy.'

I put the sponge in its place, pushed all the doubts to the back of my head and said hesitantly, 'I care for you. I don't know about marriage.'

'There is an important operation I must carry out first. I'll finish it in June. After that we can get married.'

'I don't know. What about my mother and brothers?'

'We'll send them money every month. Would your aunt and her husband take care of them?'

'I don't know.' I kept repeating that phrase like a parrot. I wanted him, but I was afraid of losing him too. 'I want to do the exam.'

'You've enough time for that. Eman, I can't and won't leave the West Bank. Please, bring your family

232

and come this summer.'

'I'll think about it. Is what you're going to do dangerous?'

'Living under the Zionists' heels is always dangerous.'

'Oh, Shadeed. If anything happens to you I'll never forgive myself.'

'I'll be all right. I promise.' He touched my hair and murmured, 'Eman,' then pulled me to him. He kissed my nose, cheeks, ears. 'Have mercy, Shadeed.' He went on kissing me. 'Please, stay.' He unbuttoned my shirt and brushed my breasts with his face. 'No, no.' I pushed him gently. My hands were trembling and pushing him was too much of an effort for me. He shut his eyes, then took a deep breath. 'I love you so much. I don't want to let you go.'

'I have to go,' I said and urged him through into the sitting room. His mother was drowsing on her mat. She opened her eyes and said, 'God lengthen your life, Eman. God give you happiness.'

'Will you excuse me, please. I have to go back to Um-Ahmad's. Tomorrow we're leaving for Rahmah.'

'God be with you.'

I kissed her wrinkled cheek and said, 'Good-bye, mother.'

'Good-bye. You must come back.'

I looked at Shadeed and said, 'Yes, mother, I will come back.'

He took my hand and walked me back. 'I'll wait for you, love.'

'Yes, I'll come back. I'll bring my mother and brothers. I'll introduce you to her and the three buds, Bakir, Omar and Malik. You know, Omar reads the paper now. I hope Malik is all right. They made fun of him at school.'

'I'll wait for you.'

I hugged him and said, almost crying, 'Shadeed, take good care of yourself. I promise you that I won't let any other man touch me. I love you.' My tears ran wildly. Love and tears. Tears and love. No rules.

He kissed both palms with his warm lips. 'Whatever happens, you will always be here,' he pointed at his heart, 'and here,' he pointed his finger at his head.

David had never been to see Shadeed in the wards.
He walked briskly to ward number 7. 'Please unlock
the door for me,' he asked the guard. Five faces
stared at him. 'Hullo,' he said, 'Where is Shadeed?'

'Shadeed the ant?' said one of them. 'He's in his
nest.'

'The blanket at the far end of the room moved.
'Shadeed, Shadeed.' He stuck his head out, shut his
eyes, opened them and joggled his head. 'Do you
remember me?'

He smiled and said, 'Mmm. You're my father. My
real father.'

'Listen to that – his real father!' shouted the same
prisoner who had spoken before.

'Shut up, Khalid.' David recognized Dirar's voice.

Shadeed pulled his hand out from under the
blanket and said, 'Look at this drawing. It's my latest
creation.'

'It's lovely, my boy.'

'A painting of us. I'll give it to her when it's
finished.'

'She's lucky to have you.'

'Where have you been all this time?'

'I spent the weekend in the Gaza Strip.'

Shadeed ran to his nest at a gallop, pulled out a
shirt with his teeth and threw it down at David's feet.

'The teacher gave me a star. They said, "Good boy". Good boy!'

'You *are* a good boy.'

'Heh, heh.' He smiled stupidly. What had happened to Shadeed's eyes that used to sparkle with intelligence? Where was the proud young man whom he knew so well? His head became lighter when he remembered the young and enthusiastic Shadeed. He straightened his collar to check that train of thought.

Khalid shouted, 'You did that to him! You kill the victim and then come to his funeral. He's quiet now, but wait till the sun starts boiling in his head, or when he shits all over the place.'

David closed his ears with his fingers. He had enough nightmares of his own.

'Khalid, we don't want any trouble.' One of the others stretched his arm to David. He shook his hand.

Shadeed said, 'Husam. I know his name. He's my teacher.'

Husam said in a low voice, 'Look at us. One is mad. Another not far from it. A broken commander, a fanatic Muslim, a radical communist and a lost anarchist.'

Shadeed pulled at David's hand to attract his attention and said, 'Father, she comes to take me every day. So beautiful. She'll drag the sun out of me. It hurts when it comes.'

'My poor boy,' he said and sat down on the floor with them.

'We are your victims,' said Husam quietly.

'No. This is our country. We had been hounded for long enough. We had to come back here.'

'This land wasn't empty. I was born here, like my father and grandfather.'

David rubbed Shadeed's back and said, 'The Arab occupation had ended.'

236

'We lived here for more than two thousand years. Do you expect us to leave now?'

'When I came from Poland, the place was empty.'

'The Palestinians had been either expelled or massacred. Haven't you seen any houses, villages of plantations?'

David remembered the citrus plantation in Gaza and the old Arab. Husam was right, but he wouldn't admit it.

Shadeed's body started jerking and he banged his head on the wall. David tried to stop him from hurting himself, but he pushed him away. Blood ran across his face. David couldn't believe his eyes. The bright boy had been reduced to a tiny ant. His whip. What had he done? What had he done? He shook his hands. Damn it. He didn't see Shadeed's blood on the cloth he was frenziedly wiping his fingers with. Finally, he screamed, 'Thirsty!' David brought him a glass of water and helped him drink it.

'Watch the thriller,' said Khalid.

Shadeed collapsed and said, 'Tired.' David helped him lie down.

'Are you happy now?' asked Khalid sarcastically.

Happy? The kid must be joking. He would leave that damned prison a few hours later and never come back. He gave Shadeed some chocolates and said to him, 'Take good care of yourself, my lad. Do whatever your brothers tell you.' Shadeed joggled his head but said nothing.

'I'll give her some chocolates. Tra-la-la.'

David looked around at the inmates. One was reading the Qur'an, another was lying down. Dirar was writing, Khalid covered his head with the blanket and Husam gave him a long quizzical look. 'Good-bye,' he whispered.

'For Palestine, our country, nothing is too dear.'

It was David's country, and whatever happened they would never leave it. The Jews had suffered enough. The amount of happiness in this world was limited, fixed. To be happy, you had to wrench some away from another person. But he didn't want to have to wrench anything away from anybody.

When he entered the interrogation room, the senior officer asked, 'Where have you been? The chief wants to see you.' See him? Why? Maybe he had heard about his frequent visits to the prisoner. God damn it, he might kick him out and he would lose the pension money. He relied on that sum of money he would receive at the end of each month. As he walked to the head office, he realised that he wouldn't care if they asked him to leave. He was leaving anyway. But the money: he needed the money. The Honda-Civic glided in front of him on the horizon. Royal-blue. Metallic. Finesse. It glowed in the sunset like a sublime sculpture. Blue and orange. He needed the money. He had responsibilities. After all, he was a father now. Would the major punish him for collaborating with the terrorist? Was that what he had done? Sure, he'd sympathized with him silently . . .

He gave the secretary a military salute. 'I believe the chief wants to see me.'

'For God's sake, where have you been? He's been asking about you every five minutes.' So the major was in one of his rages. He tried to stand steadily.

'Sir, Private first class David Dzentis is here.'

'Send him in.'

David heard the sound of trumpets as he marched into the major's office. He gave him a shaky salute.

'Sit down, soldier.'

He sat down and tried to stop his legs from shaking. Martial law was very strict: no mercy. They could easily send him to prison. Major Shlomo hemmed. The collar of his uniform was red. Red collars scared him. They filled his heart with reverence. 'How are you, soldier?'

'I'm all right, sir, thank you.'

'Still no children?'

238

Tell him. Tell him. His heart might become softer. 'My wife is pregnant, sir.'

'Congratulations. More hands to serve this young country, eh? Soldier, we are promoting you to staff sergeant.'

He hadn't grasped the words properly, but he was sure that he'd caught the word 'promotion'. 'Promoted?'

'Yes. You deserve it, soldier. Your record is clean. No trouble . . . he obeys orders and does his duty . . . satisfied with his good behaviour!'

The promotion he had been waiting for. It was unbelievable.

'First thing tomorrow morning, I want to find you here. You will be given your new uniform and a small office will be prepared for you.'

'Yes, sir. Tomorrow morning, sir.'

'Congratulations, Private, I mean Staff Sergeant.'

He jumped to his feet and said, 'Thank you, sir.' He banged the floor with his boots, gave the major a crisp salute and left his office. Outside he took his sunglasses and fixed them firmly on his nose. The prison yard looked so barren. When he took over, he would make sure that something was planted there. They would try nisanit. It would survive the heat since it was a desert flower, and practical too, because it took so deep a hold in the ground that it couldn't be rooted out. On the white flagstaff above the prison roof the flag with its star would flutter above a field of nisanit blossoms.

I went back to Rahmah and fell into a routine of work and study. Shadeed had promised to send me a letter as soon as he finished the operation. Waiting for that piece of paper was like visiting hell every morning. I walked on thorns all day long and at the end of the day I fell into an exhausted sleep, bleeding inwardly. The exam was a distraction, but it didn't stop me from thinking about the lovely months I spent with Shadeed in Nablus. I started studying six hours a day, from five to eleven, in order to pass. It was my gift to my father, my mother and Shadeed. Time became lighter, whenever I spread my books on the decaying kitchen table. Out of nowhere, Shadeed's face would appear and sit down on the page I was reading.

One night, the house was so quiet that I felt it was deserted and covered with dust. The only light in the kitchen was that of my table lamp and beyond that extended darkness. I looked out of the window at the formidable mountains. The peaks seemed like the bills of prey birds. My heart fluttered in my chest and fear hit my feet and made them limp. Something bad must have happened to Shadeed. I wished that I were no longer on my own in this world and that I could ask for help and support. I put the cup of coffee on the table, covered my face with my hands and began crying.

When I told my mother about Shadeed, she welcomed the idea of going to Nablus. 'Eh, the good old days. Your father used to take me there every Friday.'

'Have you tasted Sheikh Masaud's konaffeh?'

'Of course, my darling.'

That night she heard me crying and trudged to her chair in the kitchen. I sat down on the floor and leant on her legs. She ran her thin fingers through my hair and added my pain to her old pain that still welled up. She knew what I was going through and understood. 'Don't worry, love. He'll be all right.' I hugged her legs and started crying again. July and still no news.

I passed my exam and saw Shadeed smiling at me. 'Well done, sad eyes.' My father was standing right behind him. 'Well done, princess.' My happiness was blunted by the heavy waiting. I got a job as a teacher in an UNRWA school.

The first day of work was unforgettable – like a national feast for the neighbourhood or even a wedding. When I woke up in the morning my mother was standing over my head. 'Mother?'

'Yes, I wanted to make sure that you woke up on time, darling.'

I smiled and kissed her hand. 'Most beautiful mother in the world, you should be in your bed.'

'Not today.' She sat on the bed and watched me get dressed with a strange joy in her eyes. When I went to the kitchen to have my breakfast, she followed me there too. She straightened my collar for me as if I were a child. 'Thank God, I've seen you a teacher before I die.'

Um-Musaad dashed in through the door and said, 'Where is she? I made the bus driver wait for her at the bus-stop. We don't want her to be late on her first day, do we?'

'Ok, let's go.' Poor Habub. Shamma'eh was waiting for me too: 'Good morning, *Th*weet Eman.'

'Hello, gorgeous.'

'You're a teacher now. Don't forget to tell your *th*tuden*th* about the garbage in the *th*ity.'

'No, I won't.' I laughed and ran to the bus stop with Um-Musaad. Habub's patience was running out and with his sharp horn he woke up the whole area. When I sat down on the seat, Um-Musaad barked at Habub, 'You can go now.'

'Sir,' he said and started the engine.

It was a short walk from the bus-stop to the school. I had dreamt about that moment for years. We pass our lives grasping at slippery wishes, and when we finally catch one, what happens? Nothing. I was sure that the people of the neighbourhood were happier than I was that I had become a teacher. It was a winding road and we kept walking. I knocked on the headmistress's door.

'Come in,' a stern voice answered.

I pushed the door open and she greeted me, knotting her eyebrows. 'Eman Saqi, isn't it?'

'Yes, that's right.'

'Please, sit down.' I sat on one of the worn-out chairs. She was a soft woman who tried to wear a robe of steel.

'We will give you the first grade – it's the easiest. In our school, Eman, we insist on good behaviour in order to set a shining example to the students. If we want to teach them good manners we must first be well-mannered ourselves. In the classroom, there are three important No's: no politics, no religion, no sex.'

'Three No's?'

'You must not, I repeat, you must not talk about those three topics in the classroom.'

Shamma'eh wanted me to tell them about the garbage and it was forbidden to do so.

'I'll take you to the class you'll teach.' We walked together in an almost bare corridor, then went into one of the rooms. The boys and girls, who were playing together, jumped to their desks when they saw us. 'Good morning,' said the headmistress.

'Good morning, teacher,' they sang together.

'This is your new teacher, Miss Eman. She'll replace Miss Thuria because she is expecting.' They giggled. 'Hey, boy,' she said to one of them, 'stop it . . . I'll leave you with them, Eman.'

I wanted to memorise their names as soon as possible. 'We will start today with something light.' They listened carefully to every word I said. They were like a dry sponge, eager to absorb anything. I enjoyed the power that gave me, but at the same time I was frightened. 'I want you to tell me the meaning of your names.'

A small girl sitting in the front lisped, 'My name *ith*, er, Reem and it mean*th* deer.' The boy sitting next to her said, 'Mine is Heithm and it means the son of the eagle. And yours, Miss?'

'My name is Eman and it means faith.'

'Miss Faith, Miss Faith. Can we call you Miss Faith?'

'You just did.' The class laughed at Heithm.

After one hour of talking about names I discovered that most of the students didn't know the meaning of their names, and some even hated their names without knowing what they meant. We come into the world and then we are given names that are stuck on us like patches. Looking at their beaming faces, I wished that those blossoming buds would not go through what I went through when I was a child. At the end of the lesson I said, 'See you tomorrow.'

'*Tho*, you're coming tomorrow, Mi*th* . . . Mi*th* Faith.'

'Yes, I'm coming tomorrow.'

Um-Masaad was waiting for me in the kitchen when I arrived home. 'Was Habub waiting for you at the bus-stop?'

'Yes, he was. Please, leave the poor driver alone.'

'Give me your programme and I'll set him a schedule to go with it. He will take you and bring you back.'

My mother came into the kitchen. 'I've cooked stuffed aubergine and courgette. What do you think?'

'Fantastic.'

'How was your day?'

'I'll enjoy teaching those kids.'

'Was the headmistress nice to you?' asked Um-Musaad.

'Yes, she was.'

My brothers rushed into the kitchen and I helped them to take off their uniforms. They went to the sink and washed the backs of their hands only, so I pointed at their dirty hands and said, 'Oh, no. Wash your hands properly.' They consulted each other and said together, 'No.'

'Yes.'

'No.'

I chased them round the kitchen, laughing. They finally gave in and washed their hands again. We sat around the table. Um-Musaad was there, of course. They banged the table with their spoons: 'We want food.'

'All right, all right,' said my mother and brought the pot. I asked them if they liked it and they answered, 'Yaaa.' When I saw Malik gulping down the food I remembered Shadeed. I choked and left the table.

Their noise subsided. 'I don't know why he doesn't send her that bloody letter,' I heard Um-Musaad saying.

'Tell us about Shadeed,' asked Bakir and Malik one day. Talking about him was like adding logs to a smouldering fire, but I couldn't disappoint the beaming faces.

'Shadeed is a fedayee fighting the Zionists.' They listened spellbound. 'He is dark and lean. Very strong but gentle at the same time. When he finishes the operation we'll all go to the West Bank to see him.'

'Will he kill lots of Zionists?'

'Perhaps, yes.'

'Good. He's a hero then like daddy,' said Bakir.

'But I hate killing and blood, Eman,' said Malik. He gazed at me and I realized that the idea scared him.

'Love, I hate blood too.'

Um-Musaad rushed thorough the door one morning. 'I went to the post office today – by chance, mind you – and brought you this letter. Sharsher, the boy who works there, told me that it came through the Cross Red.'

I snatched the letter from her hand laughing. 'It's the Red Cross, Um-Musaad.'

'Whatever.'

I tore the envelope with shaking fingers and when I saw that it was *not* from Shadeed I felt so cold, as if an avalanche had slid down and carried me with it to a whitish nowhere. It was from Um-Ahmad, Sammah's aunt.

My sister, Eman,
Steadfastness is part of every Palestinians's life, especially if he is a member of the P.L.O. This

applies to his family and loved ones too. I don't know how to put this. The Zionists captured Shadeed and killed two of his brothers. They say that he is in solitary confinement. There is a rumour that he has gone mad. The sources of the Resistance Movement confirmed that. I am sorry, my daughter. What can we do? It's our destiny. You must continue the struggle. Never give up. Hand in hand, we shall return.

Your sister,
Um-Ahmad.

Everything around me stood still. I stared at the table but I couldn't see a thing. I tried to draw a breath of air. My head grew lighter and lighter until I fell down to the ground.

When I woke up, I couldn't guess where I was. Where in hell was I? I saw Um-Musaad's face. She read verses of the Qur'an over my head and blew on my face. Hanin was howling in the corner and my mother stood near the bed like a withered tree. I remembered the jumping letters and buried my face in the pillow. The flesh around my ribs hurt me. I wanted that cage to explode and let go of my heart. 'Shadeed, Shadeed,' I moaned in a dwindling voice. Even Um-Musaad collapsed crying. Shadeed, Shadeed. The whole universe shrank to a tight space. Too tight for me to breathe. Hanin pulled me to her bosom. 'The soul of your aunt, the heart of your aunt.' Shadeed.

'Oh God,' My mother wailed, 'I don't want to lose her. Two are enough. Um-Musaad, please bring Dr. Alam.'

After three days of swimming in a murky ocean, I woke up to a blackish consciousness. People moving around me were just melting shadows. Shadeed, please forgive me. Was it my fault? Shadeed, my love, please forgive me. I made out the shadow of Malik jumping into the bed. He raised his green plastic sword and sang: '"I am the savage beast, the barrel of explosives. I am the anger of the deprived, the son of the martyr, I am the son of the hero." Come to think of it, you are the daughter of the hero too.' I took him in my arms and began weeping. His eyes shone with excitement and his wet hair was dishevelled.

'Malik, love, bring me your comb.'

The next day my students came to visit me carrying a bunch of flowers. They sat in a circle around me. Everything in the room was either grey or black except the beaming faces of my six-year-old students. 'We missed you, Miss.' one of them said shyly.

'I missed you too.'

My mother offered them sweets and said, 'You're a popular teacher.' The patient bundle of bones was trying hard to drag me back to life. I smiled and said, 'Yes, most beautiful mother in the world.'

Her eyes glistened with tears. 'What a lovely morning,' she said.

'Hey, hey, hey. Ha, ha, ha. *Th*weet Eman i*th* going to work,' Shamma'eh said when he saw me that morning.

'Yes, Shamma'eh. What can I do?'

'Very wi*th*e. If you give up they will crush you.'

'What's burning my heart is what happened to Shadeed.'

'Fil*th*. That'*th* it. Wherever you have garbage you get a filthy *th*ity full of black *th*ack*th*. It'*th* a*th* *th*imple a*th* that.'

'Shamma'eh, do you think they tortured him?'

'It'*th* part of the filth.'

'Oh, Shamma'eh . . . Oh, I wish . . .'

'I wish I could get married, but wishe*th* and garbage don't go together.'

'You will, one day,' I said to him and had a feeling that he would outlive us all.

'Have you heard the late*th th*ong?'

'No.' He wanted me to ask him to sing. 'What is it?'

> They clo*th*ẹd the door,
> And prevented me from *th*eeing you.
> They didn't know that if your fa*the* di*th*hap-
>   pear*th*.
> I can *th*ee with my heart.'

'What a stupid song!'

'I've another one:

> 'My country, my country,
> Where the prophe*tth* had lived,
> Where the faithful had lived.
> Greet the time'*th* freedom fighter*th*.'

He scratched his bald head and said, 'I want to dan*the*.' He shook his waist. A scarecrow on a windy day. '*Th*mile for the garbage*th th*ake.'

I smiled.

'What a lovely day!'

Our neighbourhood, which still had no telephones, became more crowded than before. The rooms piled on top of each other like worms. The sun crept to its place in the sky. I heard a baby crying and remembered Amal. I lost them. I lost them all. I walked to the bus-stop. My feet sank in the mud of the alley. The houses were still teeming with children. In Palestine too, the camps teemed with children. I took the bus and watched the sky looking for migrating birds. Since the birds flew over Rahmah, that meant that we existed on the map. I grabbed the folder and walked to the school.

'Good morning,' I said to the eager faces.

'Good morning, teacher.'

Their voices stung me. I felt like turning my back on them and crying. Mahmud, one of my students, asked, 'Miss, how can I write "head"?' I smiled at him and said, 'I'll teach you.'

Walking back home, I tried to convince myself that there was nothing wrong in starting again from scratch. The hardest thing was to begin.

'Hello, *th*weet Eman!' said Shamma'eh and smiled, exposing his bare gums.

'Hello, gorgeous!'

Tomorrow will be better than today, Shadeed said. I felt his warm hands pulling me towards him and remembered his last words: 'You will always be here,' he said, pointing his finger at his head.

When he woke up, he found himself in Dirar's lap. 'It's better for you to stay away from me, Dirar. The sun will soon start boiling. I can feel it.' Bubble, bubble. 'Listen, the flames are eating my head. She promised that she would pull it out of me. I wish . . .' Knock on the door. Knock on the door and fill the space. 'Oh, Dirar, I'm exhausted.' His forehead was covered with sweat. The heat was unbearable. He flung the blanket on the floor and said, 'Damp place.' Dirar carried him and helped him sit down in the murky water. He shuddered, but nothing would stop the scalding pain. 'Water. Thirsty.' Dirar brought a bucket of water and poured it over his head. He gulped the glass of cold water Dirar offered him. He started screaming, then banged his head on the wall. 'Leave me alone!' he shouted, then covered his face and began crying like a baby.

'Don't cry, Shadeed. Please don't cry.'

'Your Lord has not forsaken you, nor has He become displeased. And surely what comes after is better for you than that which has gone before,' Rawhi recited.

He saw the long legs approaching, so he crawled to his nest. He was sure that they wanted to kill him. To step on him. No. He stared at the giant with his bulging eyes. 'I'll sting you,' he hissed, 'It's poisonous.'

'Husam, I've finished writing,' he said.

'Splendid, Shadeed, you're top of the class.'

Khalid shouted, 'Please throw him out. I'm going nuts.'

'Shut up, Khalid,' roared Dirar.

Khalid was crying and shaking in a white cloud. He didn't understand.

'Next time, Shadeed, I'll give you a star. Where will I stick it? Why don't you wear a shirt?'·

He joggled his head and said, 'The sun. I'll try.' He sat with them and began repeating,

'I'll write your name, my country,
On the sun that will never set.
Neither my money nor my children,
My love. No love but yours.'

When he heard the word 'sun', he ran back to his nest. Enemy number one. That shitty bellydancer.

Dirar asked, 'Why did you leave the class?'

'I hate the sun.'

'Come back. They won't repeat it again.'

He crawled back and sat alert.

Husam said to Tawfiq and Rawhi, 'Our revolution must go on. We must never give up.'

Khalid stuck his head out from under the blanket. 'Bullshit.'

'Whatever they do to us or our brothers, we must go on struggling.'

'Say hello to the noon stars,' shouted Khalid.

'The Secret High Committee of prisoners is planning a hunger strike. Of course, I sent them our support.'

'Count me out,' said Khalid.

'You'll take part even if I have to stick a knife in your side for twenty-four hours,' said Dirar.

Rawhi asked, 'If someone dies, is it considered suicide? What is the Islamic decree?'

'Rubbish,' hissed Shadeed.

'Sweet, honey,' said Husam.

Rawhi said, 'I am serious.'

'I don't know, but we'll send a letter to the High Committee.'

'Which organization is behind the strike?' asked Tawfiq.

'Does it matter? We're all members of the P.L.O.'

Shadeed hissed, 'I am a member of the P.L.O. too.' His world was dripping with pride when he said those words. Although he was only an insect, he belonged to the same organization as those giants.

Husam said, 'You know, my brother, if I could give you my eyes I would not hesitate.'

Sometimes, he did not understand. He joggled his head.

Tawfiq said, 'Revolution until victory.'

He leaned on the wall. Were they still in the cave? Had they drowned? The cloud had eaten up all his memories too. What had happened to them? What had happened to him? The glittering windows invaded his vision. The green meadows and the anemones. The sun sank behind the mountains. It stirred inside his head. Please, no. The steam poured out of his nose and ears. The bubble of boiling liquids. 'Uh.' The glare blinded him and he started crying. 'Dirar, thirsty,' he said while pressing his skull with his front leg.

'Take the pill, Shadeed – quickly.'

He took it and drank the water. His body became a piece of ash, glowing, smouldering, then the boiling stopped. His father, not his real father, was chasing him. Do you have sailors, captain? Dark and limping, captain? The sea is shit. The white kaftans raised

252

their tiny feet in the air. Blood. Blood. Rewriting history. Kill them. Where was his scout's knife? The whole class went to a picnic. Survival methods. Stone the steel-helmeted soldiers that patrol the streets. Sheikh Masaud had died, God bless his soul. His father's friend. Ya Ya Ya. Fit his feet in that hole. Mother, where are you? They would push him. The blood made their fluffy hair stick to their heads. The hollow shrieks.

'The red flag emerged, emerged.'

'And whoever does not believe in Allah and His Apostle, then surely we have prepared burning fire for the unbelievers.'

'The army of the peasant and the labourer . . .'

'Or do those in whose hearts is a disease think that Allah will not bring forth their spite?'

'I will set up a Doshka in the neighbourhood.'

'Seize him, then drag him down into the middle of hell; Then pour over his head the torment of the boiling water.'

'Welcome, welcome, Guevara.'

The Democratic State of Israel – Beer Sheva – 1985

Occupied Palestine – Beer Al-Sab'a – 1985

The breeze of the electric fan hit David's face. He sat down behind his desk and picked up a sealed envelope. It was for that poor bastard. From his sweetheart? Jud had asked him to go with her to buy a baby carriage. She wanted a dark blue one. He put the envelope in his pocket, collected his keys and went to ward No. 7. When the guard saw him, he gave him a military salute. 'Open the door, soldier.' He went in and saw Shadeed in his 'nest'.

'I have something for you.'

'What?' he said and joggled his head.

'A letter from your sweetheart.' David gave it to him and said to the guard, 'Treat that mad boy well.' The guard clenched his fist and said, 'Of course, sir.' The guard misunderstood what he'd said. Jud would be waiting. He put on his sunglasses and rushed to the car. He must hurry.

Rahmah, June 1985

My love, Shadeed,

I miss you and count the heavy days until I see you. Please answer this letter. Send me a blank sheet of paper – better than nothing. My love, I am still waiting for you no matter how long it takes. The days are bearable but darkness makes my fears worse, as well as making me long for you all the more.

My love, mother sends you her kisses, Hanin too. By the way, she is pregnant. Yassin is so happy that he can't keep his feet on the ground. Um-Musaad sends you her love too. Also Bakir, Omar and Malik, who doesn't stop talking about you and wants a picture of you. Even Shamma'eh, the garbage collector, sends you his love and says, 'Don't worry. He'll be redundant soon.' I don't know what he means by that.

Love, I have heard that the cells are cold. Please, ask the guard for an extra blanket and wrap yourself up. I want you to take good care of yourself. They told me all sorts of things about you, but I don't believe any of that rubbish.

By the way, I passed the exam and I am now teaching first grade in an UNRWA school. You should see how eager my students are. I'll come to the West Bank as soon as I can get leave. I'll ask your mother to come with me to Rahmah. I am sure she will enjoy the company of my mother and Um-Musaad. What do you think? I will ask her.

I've grown thinner lately, It's womanhood, they say. Do you mind, love?

I hope to see you soon.

    Love,
    Eman.

He tightened his eye muscles and looked at the paper. Why did they give him that crap? He was so angry, he wanted to slash a part of his body. Hit his head. Hurt himself. Hurt them. He squatted, urinated, then emptied his bowels. He blinked, joggled his head, then wiped his arse with the paper.

'He hasn't done that before,' remarked Dirar.

'He's becoming more civilised,' said Khalid.